# ONE LETTER

**MARCIE STEELE**

Pink Coffee Pot Press

# THREE YEARS AGO

Rose Pritchard took her seat on the front pew of Somerley Church. She and her husband weren't regular churchgoers, but they had come there to celebrate many friends and family over the years. Their daughter, Eve, had married there; their granddaughter, Grace, was christened. Several of their friends had been buried in the nearby cemetery. Now she was saying goodbye to Harry.

She didn't hate the man lying in the coffin, well, not entirely. But she hadn't had the life with him that she'd envisioned. Harry had died two weeks ago. He'd been seventy-six, the same age as Rose, a ripe old age, some would say. An illness over his last years had marred what had been left for him.

The whole marriage had done that to Rose.

She glanced around, noting friends who'd come to pay their respects. Mr and Mrs Carmichael from the golf club. Sheena from the café on the high street, and George and Stanley from the Hope and Anchor pub. Their neighbour, Alf. Her friend, Iris. Sally Armstrong, from the charity shop.

Sally was dabbing at her eyes with a handkerchief, a

younger woman Rose didn't know trying to comfort her. Rose always suspected Harry had more than a soft spot for Sally, but she'd had no real evidence. Just a woman's intuition.

Behind them were more people of Somerley. She expected Harry would be pleased that so many of his friends were here.

Once the first hymn, "Abide with Me," was sung, Reverend Michaels took his place at the lectern and spoke about Harry and their life together as a family. There were smiles, and a little light laughter, as he shared anecdotes Rose had told him about when they'd arranged the funeral the week before.

'Harry was a pillar of the community,' he went on. 'Admired by many for his kind nature. He would go out of his way to help anyone.'

Rose turned her head to the left, catching Eve's eye. Only the two of them knew what the real Harry was like. The one who was sadistic behind closed doors. The one who had enjoyed being in control.

Even though her partner, Liam, was standing next to her, Grace was sobbing into her dad's chest. Clark was soothing her as best he could.

Rose gave a faint smile. It must be hard for Grace. Harry had never shown his nasty streak to his granddaughter. Grace, thankfully, had been spared. She thought her granddad was being funny all the time, laughing with her gran, not laughing at her, as had been the case. It was easy enough to fool her because Rose had laughed along, too, for the most part.

Rose had been pleased when Eve married Clark. He was nothing like Harry, and she knew he took care of Eve well. Clark encouraged her to grow, something Harry had never endorsed. His views had been old-fashioned. A woman's place was in the home, no matter how much they tried to bring him into the twenty-first century.

Rose blamed the generation she'd been born into. Harry's

parents had brought their son up in an environment where the man had ruled the house, and the woman was there to wait on him and their children. Harry had been an only child, a spoilt one at that. Rose had long thought he'd wanted a mother rather than a wife. Someone to attend to his needs, other than to love him.

Prayers were said, then the notes to the next hymn were played on the organ, and everyone stood up. Rose felt Eve's hand in her own and squeezed it, thankful for her support.

And then it was over. Once she had got through the wake, there would be no more pretence required. She could close the door on her home in Hope Street and do whatever she liked.

She took a final look at the coffin. At the last minute, she hadn't put the letter she'd written into the pocket of Harry's suit. Even so, it had been a relief to write out all her feelings and then throw the letter away. Cathartic, too, like seeing a therapist. Washing her hands of her problems once they'd been aired, with no harm done to anyone else.

That was one thing about Rose.

She could never be as cruel as Harry.

# CHAPTER ONE

Eve Warrington wrung out the dishcloth as if she was trying to squeeze the life out of someone. There wasn't any particular reason why she felt the need to be so harsh, but still. She ran it across the worktop, washing away the detritus from the previous day.

It was half past seven. Somerley Heights was mostly quiet as she went about her morning shift. First the ground floor and then working her way up to the next one.

She enjoyed her job for the most part, especially when the weather was as glorious as it was now. Sun streaming in through the windows was always better than seeing rain pouring down. It lifted her spirits, helping her to stop overthinking everything.

'Morning, Eve.' An elderly man walking towards her raised a gnarly hand. 'Beautiful day, isn't it?'

Eve glanced up to see him almost at her feet. It didn't matter that he was still in his pyjamas and dressing gown as he was in the communal corridor. His wispy white hair was combed down, and he had bushy eyebrows that she longed to trim. A right old Santa Claus in the making.

'Morning, Edward.' She smiled. 'Yes, I hope it holds out. I have washing on the line.'

'How's Rose? I haven't seen her in a while.'

'She's very well, thank you.'

'Tell her I was asking after her.'

'I will.' Eve knew he was on his way downstairs to collect his morning paper that was dropped off by the local newsagent. Even so, she counted in her head as he went past. She'd reached three before Edward turned back to her.

'Have you been to my flat yet?' he asked.

'Not yet, Edward.'

'Well, when you do, please be careful of Molly. She doesn't like strangers.'

'I'll be sure to remember that.'

Her answer seeming to satisfy him, she smiled to herself when Edward shuffled along on his travels. Eve didn't clean the flats. It was her job to keep the communal areas spick and span. And Molly? Well, she'd been Edward's dog. She'd died last year and, due to his dementia, some days he didn't even remember that he'd had a dachshund. So Eve humoured him, agreeing with whatever he said about Molly on a daily basis. It was kinder that way.

An hour later, she'd finished her shift and stored away her cleaning paraphernalia. She closed her locker with a sigh, shoulders sagging in relief. Then she left the staffroom and headed upstairs to see her mum. At flat number twelve, she let herself in and knocked on the door.

'Hello, are you decent?' she cried.

'Well, if you count me wearing cheap knickers rather than my usual M and S, then yes.'

Eve chuckled, going into the living room. Rose was sitting on the settee, dressed and made up. Her thick white hair, her crowning glory, was styled in a bob with a blunt fringe. Brown eyes twinkled beneath hooded lids, and she smiled at Eve.

The TV was showing a documentary on a craft shop. Eve stopped to watch for a few seconds. But when Rose reached for the remote, Eve held up the bag in her hand.

'Don't mind me. I've just brought your shopping.'

'Thanks, love.' Rose got to her feet and followed Eve into the kitchen. Units on both sides had created a galley, barely big enough for one person to stand in the middle, let alone two. But the walls were freshly painted every year, and Rose was a stickler for everything being in its place.

Somerley Heights had been home for Rose since Eve's dad, Harry, had died. She'd moved out of Hope Street, just off the high street, into the retirement complex for the over sixties and, although all the properties were privately owned, there was a warden on site twenty-four hours and assisted living if needed.

Rose pushed a ten-pound note into Eve's hand.

'Mum,' Eve chided, handing it back. 'I've told you before I don't need any extra cash. You give me enough for what you need.'

'But you have to fetch it for me.'

'You can always have it ordered in.'

'And have all the sell-by dates so short that things will go off before I can eat them?'

Eve switched off as Rose had her usual rant about everything being less fresh nowadays.

'It's no trouble, Mum.'

Rose placed a hand on the side of Eve's face. 'You look tired, love.'

'I'm okay.'

'I worry about you.'

'I know.' Eve raised a smile. 'Grace sends her love. Says she'll be around this weekend.'

'I hope she's still not fretting over that loser. If I get my hands on him, I'll rip off his—'

'She hasn't seen him in a long time now, thank goodness.'

'No one else on the horizon?'

'I don't think so.'

'Honestly, the pair of you are a waste of time. You both need to find someone new to love.'

Eve switched off again. She didn't want to think about Clark right now, how she'd lost him three months after her father had died.

'Do you need anything?' she asked instead.

'I don't think so.'

At seventy-nine years of age, Rose was coping well. She had her independence, a small car to run around in, her health was as expected, and she forgot things from time to time. But Eve loved her spirit. She was a positive soul now, not like her, all Negative Nora.

Eve didn't really have to worry about money, thank goodness. The house was paid for, she had a little in the savings account, and there were few big bills now she wasn't going on lavish holidays on a regular basis. She ran a sewing and alterations business, too, that she did as and when it was required. So if she didn't spend recklessly, she would be fine until her retirement.

She straightened up after putting the groceries away, her knees cracking in complaint, and rubbed at the small of her back.

'Are you even listening to a word I'm saying?' Rose chastised.

Eve glanced round. 'Sorry, I was miles away.'

'I said there's a dishy caretaker started yesterday. He's about your age.'

'I'm fifty-four. I don't need fixing up by my mother.'

'I know, I know. I'm just saying he was very easy on the eye.'

'I thought we had a caretaker. Has he left?'

'No.' Rose frowned. 'He's the maintenance manager, that's it. He's in charge of the caretaker and the gardener and overseeing the new extension.'

Eve struggled when Rose tried to matchmake for her. If she wanted to find someone new, she would.

Trouble was, like her daughter, Eve hadn't got over losing the last man.

Eve left Rose twenty minutes later. She walked down the steps to the lobby, making a mental list of things she needed to do that morning. She wanted to strip the beds and get some more washing out on the line. There was no rain forecast, so they'd be dry in no time.

Then there was the insurance and car tax she needed to sort out. The fridge was on the blink again, although she was trying to get a few more months out of it and—

At ground level, Eve collided with a man who was backing in through the door. The box he was carrying flew out of his hands and across the foyer. A container of screws from inside it emptied all over the floor, shattering the peace.

'I'm so sorry.' Eve stooped down to help. 'It was my fault. I wasn't looking where I was going. Here, let me help.'

'No harm done; I wasn't looking either. You made me jump more than anything.'

The man was wearing a black T-shirt, stretched across a nice chest. His trousers had far too many pockets, even with the carpenter's pouch wrapped around his waist full of tools.

'Sorry, again. I was in a world of my own and I... Mack?'

The man's face changed as he recognised her, breaking out into a smile she remembered from years gone by. 'Eve Pritchard!'

'Well, yes, that was my maiden name. I'm Eve Warrington now.'

She gathered up the screws with him.

'It's good to see you.' He smiled. 'I didn't expect to bump into you here – literally.'

'I work here, cleaning for three hours each weekday morning. My mum lives in flat twelve, too. I've just come from there.'

'Ah, I remember Rose with fond memories. She was always nice to me.'

Eve smiled, pleased he'd recalled her name. 'Are you visiting someone?'

'No, I work here, too. It's my first week.'

Eve's eyes widened. 'You're the new maintenance manager?'

'That's me!'

Eve recalled what her mum had said. Rose hadn't recognised Mack, and she couldn't wait to tell her. Mind, neither of them had seen him since he was in his late teens.

There was silence while they digested everything. Once all the screws had been popped back into the container, they spoke at once.

'I'd best leave you to that,' Eve said.

'I'd better crack on,' Mack said.

They both smiled.

Eve opened the door and Mack went up to the first floor.

'Nice seeing you again,' Mack shouted over his shoulder. 'Perhaps we could catch up over a coffee in the staffroom sometime?'

'I'll look forward to it,' she replied.

Eve walked away, a smile playing on her lips. Now there was a turn up for the books, she mused, opening the side door out onto the car park.

Mackenzie Charlton. She'd had a crush on him for a few months in high school, and then they'd started dating. They'd been together for two years before he'd broken her heart and gone to university in Lancashire, leaving her behind in Somerley.

Of course she knew it wasn't that simple. She wasn't academically minded, preferring the arts to the heavier subjects. Her dad had always dissuaded her whenever she'd mentioned it anyway. Besides, she'd been happy in Somerley.

Because she'd met Clark, fallen in love, married him and, eventually, Grace had come along to make it all perfect. Life had been kind, until the day everything had changed in an instant.

# CHAPTER TWO

Grace Warrington popped her computer screen into sleep mode, grabbed her notebook and pen in one hand and her mug of coffee in the other, and went through to the meeting room for the Monday morning editorial get-together. There was only one person in there when she went in.

'Morning,' she greeted Tom as she pulled out a chair and sat across from him. 'Did you have a good evening?'

Tom was the editor of *Somerley News* and had been at an awards ceremony the night before.

'Yes. The best bit was when the waiter spilt tomato soup down the front of Phil Martin's shirt. He looked like he was playing a victim in a murder mystery.'

'Well, at least that's as dramatic as things go in Somerley. I bet you all made fun of him, though, you rotten lot.'

'We did. I asked him if he'd like bread with it.'

Grace smirked. In her opinion, it couldn't have happened to a better person. Phil Martin was a sleazebag. There had been a few occasions where he'd tried to be a little too friendly with her, and she'd had to knock him down with a curt remark. She ignored him for the most part, though.

Bizarrely, he smelt of cheese and onion crisps, no matter what time of day or evening.

Tom glanced at his watch. 'Have you seen the other two yet?'

The Features and Editorial Team was made up of Grace, Della, and Joe. Joe was in his mid-sixties and ready for retirement at the end of the year, and Grace was going to miss him. She'd known him all her life, her parents having been friends with him and his wife, Fiona. He'd also been a great mentor to her since the day she'd arrived there five years ago, showing her the tricks of the trade. There was no doubt she'd become a better journalist because of it.

Joe had been a great comfort when her dad died suddenly, too. He'd helped her to get through many working days, and she was sure when the newspaper downsized, going from five weekday editions to once a week, and staff were cut by fifty percent, that it was him who had saved her job.

Della was in her mid-thirties and was covering maternity leave for Kim Mitchell, their permanent feature writer. She'd only been there a month so far, and Grace hadn't quite got the feel of her. Della was tardy most days, and Grace knew that was getting on Tom's nerves. But she seemed to be a good feature writer and knew the town and its people well.

'Joe has a doctor's appointment first thing,' Grace rattled off. 'Della hasn't arrived yet. Shall we wait for her or get started?'

'We should crack on. I—'

'Hang on, hang on.'

Della waltzed in behind them in a skirt and top that were both far too tight, and a flurry of some overwhelming floral perfume. She sat down with aplomb, brushing brown wavy hair away from her face.

'Sorry I'm a little late.' She got out her notebook and pen, then popped on her glasses. 'I was up until the wee hours researching Sapphire Lake. It has a fascinating history, and I got carried away. I was exhausted when I got into bed and I'm afraid I overslept.'

'Well, you're here now, so we can get started.' Tom's face was unreadable. 'First on the agenda, an autumn project. I want to do something to bring the community together.'

Grace reached for a chocolate digestive from the plate in front of her. 'Somerley are a close-knit bunch already.'

'Not everyone loves this place like you.' Della laughed, rolling her eyes at Tom.

They both ignored her jibe.

'That's the same for every small market town,' Grace defended her point. 'There are always people who will join in and people who won't.'

Della paused. 'Will there be a budget?'

'A few hundred pounds I can raise by sponsorships and ads around the project. That's where you two come in, and Joe.' Tom glanced from one to the other. 'I'll let you have a think about things until Friday, and then we can see what you've all got. Della, can you bring Joe up to speed when he gets in?'

As Della nodded, enthusiasm besieged Grace. She was never very good at being put on the spot, yet this could be a chance for her to show what she was made of.

'This Friday?' She grimaced. 'That doesn't give us much time.'

'I'll be able to rattle off a few ideas by then,' Della spoke with authority.

Grace stared at Della. It was typical of her. From what she'd seen so far, Della didn't seem to be a team player, and Grace had the feeling she'd be the dogsbody again if Della was the lead on the project. Not that she expected anything else, as she was junior to both her and Joe. But she didn't want to be a feature assistant for too much longer. She wanted to be an editor, take on her own things.

Putting forward a great idea might be a way to start.

'So do you think you're up for it?' Tom asked them.

'I'll have some ideas by Friday,' Grace confirmed.

'Me, too.' Della paused. 'I've been thinking, Tom. We should have a meeting about the marketing budgets. I might have come up with an idea to save us a few pennies and I'd like to go over it with you.'

'Great.' Tom stood up to signal the meeting was over. 'Grace, will you tell Flora to book Della a slot in my diary for later in the week?'

Grace nodded, although slightly peeved about being put in her place in front of the temp.

'Plus a new project might take your mind off things,' Della said once Tom was out of hearing range, a snide look on her face.

Della was referring to Grace's four-year relationship with her ex, Liam, finishing over the spring. She chose not to snap back, unsure why Della had to be so spiteful all the time. Grace had thought they'd bonded during the first week Della had arrived, but it seemed since then, Della had used everything she'd told her to try and wind her up.

She'd been back at her desk for twenty minutes when she saw Joe arriving.

'Hey, the old man is here!' she cried, smiling as he ambled over to his desk. 'How did it go at the docs?'

'Most probably indigestion.' Joe rubbed at his chest before sitting down across from her. 'I've been given some tablets to help.'

Joe was a bear of a man in all senses of the word. With a warm personality, he was tall yet cuddly, with deep-set hazel eyes and a great head of salt-and-pepper hair. He always cheered up the day, and he gave the best of hugs.

He wheeled out a chair. 'What have I missed?'

'We're running a community project and we've all got to come up with an idea each before the meeting on Friday.'

'Sounds interesting. Have you thought of any?'

Grace's shoulders dropped. 'I've been racking my brains, but nothing's happening yet.' She passed him the remit to read.

Joe glanced over it. 'Do you have any ideas, Della?'

'Of course, but I'm not about to share them with you, until Friday.' She took out her mobile phone. 'I have to make a few calls – in private.'

'Not very much of a team player, is she?' Grace muttered to her disappearing form. 'I miss Kim. How long is it until she's back?'

'Three months, two weeks, and three days.'

'That long?' Grace rested her head on the desk.

'Ignore her. Let's think of something for you to do that will knock her ideas out of the water. What's the funding budget?'

'A few hundred.'

Joe picked up his mug. 'Make me a brew, and I'll have a think with you.'

Grace grinned. 'Deal.'

# CHAPTER THREE

Rose Pritchard relaxed back into the settee, popped her feet up on the stool, and reached for her Kindle. She was looking forward to half an hour's peace and quiet and was aiming to finish the latest Jill Mansell novel. She and her friend, Iris, had not long had a cup of tea in Iris's flat, so there wasn't much chance of being interrupted. Three chapters to go.

Rose loved using a Kindle. It was far easier for her to hold than a heavier paperback, plus she could adjust the font size, enabling her to read without too much eye strain. Over the years, she'd read at least two books a week, getting most from the local library or the charity shop on the high street.

Harry had been a tight flint and hated her spending money on luxuries, as he called them. They cost next to nothing compared to his golf equipment and annual club membership fees. As well, there was the chess club on Monday afternoons, darts at the Hope and Anchor every Tuesday and Friday evening, and the meals out with retired work colleagues that seemed to happen at least once a week. But that was Harry all over, getting his priorities right to her detriment.

Rose still couldn't believe it had been three years since he'd passed. Despite their tumultuous marriage, it had been terrible at the time to see him in so much pain. He'd been a shadow of his former self during his last months and had refused visits from everyone. Even to the end, he had been a difficult man.

And yet, she still believed in true love. Rose wanted to see her girls settled again before it was her time to leave this earth.

Eve had been widowed now for nearly as long as she had. Clark's death had come as a total shock. So unexpected and such a tragedy as they were a close couple. Eve was still lost without him, Rose could tell. But she could also see she was lonely, perhaps ready to move on and find someone new. She wouldn't blame her.

Rose missed having Clark around, too. He would always be there if she needed any odd jobs doing, changing lightbulbs, assembling flat-pack furniture. He told her the rudest of jokes full of schoolboy humour and teased her all the time, for some reason calling her Rosie Red, which she always smiled at.

He'd found Eve when she was at her lowest. Vulnerable because her first boyfriend had gone off to university and their relationship had petered out. Much to their surprise, he'd got on well with Harry.

It was easy to like Clark. Even in his twenties, he'd had a charm about him. A reassuring calm, too. Harry always seemed to be on his best behaviour around him, giving her and Eve a reprieve.

Rose remembered the first time they'd met him. Eve had been so nervous about bringing him home. But the lad had charmed the usual hard-rock exterior of her father.

Rose had cooked dinner for the four of them, and then Harry and Clark had gone for a pint at the Hope and Anchor.

Eve had been annoyed that she'd been left behind, but Rose could tell it was important to her that Clark bonded with Harry.

From the success of that evening, and the warm feelings she had for Eve and Clark becoming an item, Rose had hoped that the couple would fall madly in love, and they had. They were married two years later. The wedding had been wonderful, and one of the times where Harry hadn't been the centre of attention, although he'd tried to hog the limelight whenever he could.

But Clark had been a heavy smoker in his early days. He'd managed to give up a few years before his death, yet Rose often wondered if it had given him a helping hand into an early grave. Three months they'd been blessed with him without Harry. She had got to know him better than ever through that.

And poor Grace, Rose's little angel. Grace was the heart of their small family, despite Harry always moaning that Rose spoiled her too much. He could talk. He'd doted on Grace, and she him. Having only one daughter, a precious grandchild had been wonderful. Rose had enjoyed watching her grow up from the infant who'd entered the world screaming, to the confident beautiful woman she was today. She was such a joy to have around.

Iris had seven grandchildren and fourteen great-grandchildren at the last count. Someone was always calling round to see her. Rose wasn't sure she'd like that. She enjoyed her alone time. Even so, she couldn't wait for Grace to bear her a great-grandchild, if that was her choice in life.

When Grace had introduced her ex-boyfriend, Liam, to them, on first impressions Rose thought he was smarmy. As she'd got to know him better, he wasn't quite as bad as she'd imagined, but there was something about him she didn't like.

She'd mentioned it to Eve, who'd said she had a similar feeling.

In the end, they'd put it down to him being envious of Grace's job. Grace often had to cover events during the evening so was always getting dressed up to be wined and dined. However, the reality was, she was constantly interviewing people and writing up notes, and taking photos on her phone. She barely had time to enjoy herself.

But she loved being a social butterfly.

Liam didn't seem to like that Grace was so well-known. It was him who always wanted to be the centre of attention. But everywhere they went someone would recognise Grace and want to stop and chat. She loved it, Liam not so much.

After they'd split, Grace moved back in with Eve. She'd seemed heartbroken at first. Rose had been there for her, with a shoulder to cry on and soothing words of wisdom, all the time glad how things had panned out.

Eve had told her she liked having Grace around again. It wouldn't be forever, Grace was too independent not to strike out on her own. But, for now, the arrangement suited them both.

And it was good to see Grace back on her feet. She seemed to be finding out that life without Liam was okay.

Rose switched on her Kindle, knowing there was someone else out there for her granddaughter, someone who deserved her love much more than Liam. For Eve, too.

And, as Rose was fast approaching her eightieth birthday, she only hoped she had time to see them both settled down before anything happened to her.

# CHAPTER FOUR

On Wednesday morning, Eve had finished her shift and was enjoying a coffee before leaving. She flipped through the latest edition of *Somerley News,* searching for pieces that Grace had written. She always felt a shiver of pride whenever she saw her name on the byline, and Grace never failed to surprise her with some of the things she covered.

This week, she was on the warpath as some youths were hounding a pensioner in his home. It was an address on the outskirts of Somerley, on the large estate if she remembered rightly.

'Knock-knock.'

Eve glanced up to see Mack in the doorway, quite surprised when her stomach lurched at the sight of him. He looked fresh, clean-shaven, hair mussed from being out in the wind, no doubt.

'Hi, Mack,' she greeted.

He pointed to the newspaper. 'Any gossip in there?'

'I'm reading one of the articles my daughter has written.' Eve ran a hand through her hair, hoping her bob was still as slick as it had been that morning. 'She's been a feature assistant at *Somerley News* for a few years.'

'Ah, yes, I was shocked to see it had gone to weekly. Sign of the times, I guess. I remember when it was five days a week. It's a shame there are so many cutbacks. But then again, I suppose when we were in *the dark ages*, there was a need for a printed paper to advertise the stuff we can easily see online now.'

'Things have certainly changed since we were teens.' Eve smiled and dipped her eyes. 'Cassette tapes and CDs moving over for streaming.'

'All those TV channels when we had, what, three?'

'And black and white.'

'Mobile phones instead of taking calls in the hall with someone listening all the time.'

'And getting moaned at about the cost of us yapping all night.'

They laughed as they reminisced, although Eve remembered her dad always being the one to cut her off mid-call.

'Are you off home soon?' Mack pointed to her mug.

'Yes, but I'm going to see Mum first.' She paused. 'Would you like to see her? Do you have time?'

'Sure, I'm due a break.'

'Great.' Eve closed the newspaper and stood up. 'I can embarrass her if she doesn't recognise you.'

'Been talking about me, have you?' Mack teased.

'She told me we had a new caretaker – sorry, maintenance manager – but she didn't say it was you.'

'Ah, I answer to all sorts regardless.' He stepped to one side. 'Lead the way.'

They chatted while they walked. Eve was dying to ask a ton of questions but didn't want to seem nosy. Mack, however, wasn't backwards about coming forwards.

'So, when we bumped into each other the other day, you mentioned a change in surname?' he queried.

'Yes, I was married.'

'Ah, so you're a divorcee?'

'No, a widow.'

Mack balked. 'Me and my big mouth. I'm sorry.'

Eve waved his comment away. 'It was three years ago now. Clark and I were married for nearly thirty years. We got together quite early.' She cringed, wondering if he thought she was being antsy about their breakup.

He didn't seem perturbed. 'Yeah, it was the done thing back then, wasn't it? I reckon the divorce rate would be far less if we hadn't felt the need to conform so much.'

'My marriage was happy.'

'I meant in general!' Mack shook his head. 'What is wrong with me today? Anyway, I'm a widower, so we have one thing in common.'

'Oh, well, I'm sorry, too.' Eve's smile dropped.

'Don't be. It was a while ago now.'

As they drew level with flat twelve, there wasn't time to find out more, so she opened the door and shouted to Rose. They found her in the kitchen.

'Hi, Mum. I've brought someone with me today.'

Eve stepped aside so that Rose could see Mack behind her in the doorway.

'Oh, hello.' Rose offered her hand. 'I'm Rose, pleased to meet you.'

'You've already met him,' Eve took great pleasure in telling her.

'Have I?' Rose peered at Mack. 'Your face doesn't look familiar.'

'It was quite some time ago.' Mack chuckled. 'Me and Eve dated for a short while when we were teenagers. You used to invite me to tea, and I was grateful for everything you cooked for me. My home life wasn't great, and it was much more pleasant at your house.'

Rose's eyes dipped for a fraction of a second. Mack wouldn't have noticed, but Eve did. Mack had seen the side to her father that most people saw.

Eve stepped back in time for a moment, recalling the earlier years when she and Mack had been together. He was the youngest of six, having four sisters and a brother. She remembered him telling her how money had been tight, even more so when his dad left when he was seven. Mack's mum had then died when he was sixteen, and he'd gone to live with his eldest sister and her brood until he'd left for university.

The three of them chatted, Rose and Mack over tea, reminiscing about when Rose could remember Mack calling round. Eve couldn't help thinking the one time she wanted her mum to ask questions so she could find out more about him without seeming too inquisitive, she wasn't very helpful.

Rose was quite subdued. Had she stepped back in time, too? That wouldn't be very pleasant for her if so.

'Time for me to make a move,' Mack said, although he seemed quite comfortable on Rose's settee.

'You couldn't add my dripping tap in the bathroom to your list of jobs to do, please?' Rose gave her best encouraging smile.

Eve rolled her eyes in jest. 'Mum, what are you like?'

'It's no bother.' Mack nodded. 'Are you in this afternoon, around two?'

'I can be.'

'You're very lucky,' Eve commented. 'It isn't often I catch her in. She has more of a social life than I do.'

'Oh, behave.' Rose tittered.

Mack laughed, too. 'I'll see you then. Nice chatting to you, Eve.'

'Likewise.'

As soon as she'd closed the door behind him, Rose pounced on her daughter.

'Well, what's his story?'

'I don't know yet. We haven't chatted much. He thought I was divorced, and I told him I was widowed. He told me he was a widower, and then we got to your door.'

'Oh! Well, you'll have to do better than that. I want to know why he's back.'

So do I, thought Eve. More importantly, she wanted to know if he would be sticking around.

'I know I thought a lot of Clark, but remind me why you and Mack didn't go any further than your teens,' Rose added.

'We were into different things, I guess.'

'But you were quite an item. If I recall correctly, you thought a lot of him.'

'Until he left to go to uni.'

'Ah.' Rose grimaced. 'I remember now, I'm sorry.'

'It was a long time ago, and we were young.' It was the first thing Eve thought of saying to throw her mum off the scent, because she couldn't tell her the real reason.

That would upset her completely.

# 1964

*My dearest Rose,*

*I hope this letter finds you well. It's already a year since I last saw you. I am still missing you like crazy even so. I'm settled now, in Northumberland. I live in Hexham with my aunt. It's a beautiful village, not far from Newcastle, and I'm sure you'd love it. It reminds me of Somerley, a small-town vibe but not enough to feel claustrophobic. There's a lovely high street and lots of nice walks around its edge. I can go for miles some days and never see a soul. Perfect for a bit of peace and quiet.*

*I'm working at a new factory. It only opened a few months ago, and I'm the production manager, can you believe that? I always thought I wouldn't make much of myself and I am really enjoying it here. I've made a lot of new friends, I have a great social life, and I'm earning a good living. Life is okay.*

*Except that I wish you were here with me. It doesn't seem right without you. You're the first thing I think of when I wake each morning, and the last thing I think about before I go to sleep. I wonder if you are well, if you're happy. If you're still with Harry. I can't even be with another woman yet. My heart still belongs to you.*

*I wish I'd told you why I was leaving, rather than going with no* word. I will never know if it would have made a difference. I realise now that I was in love with you, and I should have done something about it. I should have asked if you felt the same. I think you did, but now I'll never know.

You see, I was a coward. I let fear dictate my circumstances. It was also the worry of what might happen to you if I didn't leave.

Equally, I couldn't see you in love with another man when I couldn't be by your side. Not be able to see you; not be able to kiss you. It was more than my heart could bear.

Do you ever think of me, Rose? Wonder what might have been, the way that I do? I wish things had been different. Who knows what might have happened if I'd got to speak to you before I left?

I hope one day that our paths will cross. Perhaps I'll come back to Somerley and bump into you. Maybe then I will see if you have feelings for me, too. I thought you had. I knew you had. And yet... it was only fair due to the circumstances.

I hope you are happy if you are with Harry and that he treats you well. No one deserves that more than you.

All my love,
Cedric

## CHAPTER FIVE

'Anyone fancy a cuppa?' Grace stood up and stretched her arms to the ceiling.

'Ooh, thought you'd never ask,' Della remarked, holding up her mug. 'Although don't make it as milky as last time. It was very much the consistency of cat pee.'

Grace took it from her, smiling to herself as Joe smirked when she pulled a face that Della wouldn't see.

There were eight people who worked for *Somerley News*. Along with Tom and their team, there was Ethan, who was the photography and digital production manager, Nathan and Ben who sold advertising space, and Flora, who was the admin officer, manning the reception whenever needed. With the management having cut back on staff when the paper downsized, they all mucked in to do their own layouts and typing, and daily crap as they called it.

Apart from Flora, who was seeing to someone who wanted to put an ad in this week's edition, no one else wanted a top-up. While Grace popped the various concoctions of sugar, coffee, tea, and milk in their rightful places, her mind was on the community project again. Already it was Thursday, and she hadn't come up with anything to stand out yet.

What would get the people of Somerley interested enough to join in? Could she ask them their best memories of the town through the years? Perhaps do a display in the local library. Have a coffee morning, maybe a meet-up, where residents could reminisce.

It probably wouldn't be the idea she would finish with, but it was a start. And, if she couldn't think of anything else, at least she wouldn't have a blank sheet to go into Friday's meeting with.

Another thought popped into her head. What about community awards, with a ball to announce the winners? But then, that was similar to what the local radio station did, so it was hardly unique.

She wondered what Della would come up with. Despite being part of the same team, it seemed as if a competitive nature was building between them. Except for Joe, of course, who had promised to give her his best idea. He just had to think of it first.

She dished out the drinks and, while Della had nipped to the loo, took the opportunity to run her thoughts past him.

'We've already done both of those over the years,' he said.

'I can't remember the first one.'

'You weren't here then.'

'So it was a long time ago. We can do it again.'

'Yes, if you can't come up with anything else. You know what they say. The first few ideas are the usual ones. Dig deeper and see what you come up with. I have faith in you.'

Grace pursed her lips. Maybe, but did she have faith in herself?

'What are you two wittering on about?' Della said, sitting down again moments later. 'You're always gossiping.'

'It's called mulling things over,' Joe replied. 'We do it all the time. Two heads are often better than one in this game.'

'Well, at your age, it is. It's a wonder you remember to put your teeth in every morning.' Della laughed at her joke, but when it was met with deadpan looks, she dropped her smile.

Joe remained calm, saying nothing in retaliation. But Grace could tell he was annoyed. What was wrong with Della? Surely she knew how rude she'd been.

'I don't think you should say that to Joe. I—' she started.

'I think your idea has legs, Grace,' Joe interrupted. 'Let me look at it again.'

Grace, realising his game, handed him a sheet of blank paper. Della's head had already gone down, though.

'It's a shame she's going to be around to spoil every day until I retire,' Joe muttered. 'I don't know what we did to deserve that.'

'We'll have to show her that we work as a team, Joe. We have to come up with a good project.'

'We will, you'll see.'


Rose always came to tea on Thursdays, and Eve was putting together a quick meal of pasta carbonara. Grace would be home from work soon.

It was nice to get the three of them together at the same time now that Grace had moved back in with her temporarily. She'd been living with Liam when Clark had died, and even though she'd offered to move back for a while, Eve had told her there was no need. Now, though, it was lovely having company again.

The house could be so empty, even though Grace was noisy and hogged the bathroom in the mornings. But the chatter they shared over breakfast, and watching TV together with a bottle of wine, was something she was really enjoying.

The back door opened.

'Only me!' Rose came through to the kitchen. She put down her keys and handed Eve a carrier bag. 'I bought a mocktail for us.'

'Thanks.' Eve popped the bottle into the fridge to chill. 'I won't be long with this. Grace will be here any minute. She has a project she needs some help with.'

'Oh?' Rose pulled out a chair and sat down.

'She'll tell you when she gets here.'

'Now you have me intrigued.'

'It's a—'

'Are you two talking about me?' Grace walked in.

'Yes,' they replied in unison.

Grace bent down to kiss her gran on the cheek.

'Your mum says you want to chat about your community project,' Rose said.

Grace's shoulders sagged. 'There might not be one if I can't come up with the best idea. This could be my chance to shine, and yet I can't think of anything with oomph.'

'I'm sure you will,' Eve insisted. 'It'll probably come to you when you least expect it.'

'I have to have something for the meeting tomorrow!' Grace held up her notebook. 'Can I run a few things past you both, that I'd love some advice on?'

'Of course. Sit down and we'll see what we can do.'

Grace went through the ideas she'd written down as Eve dished out the food and, before they'd begun to eat, either her mum or her gran dismissed them one by one as too simple or overdone.

Grace groaned. 'You've said the same as Joe when I showed him the list.'

'What about doing something with a positive angle?' Rose queried.

'I thought any community project would be that.' Grace looked confused.

'I mean something all ages will want to join in. People are so pessimistic nowadays. I wonder....' Rose put down her cutlery and then shook her head. 'No, that's a silly idea.'

'I'll take anything right now,' Grace said. 'Go on.'

Rose wiped her mouth with a napkin. 'How about mixing the old with the new? You young ones are all text messages and scrolling on gadgets with screens nowadays.'

'Says the woman who's never without her iPad,' Eve admonished.

'That's true.' Rose laughed. 'Where would I be without it? It has everything at my fingertips. But, back in my day, as I've said lots of times.'

'*Lots* of times,' Grace teased.

'Back in my day,' Rose repeated, 'we had to communicate the old-fashioned way. Writing letters. Why not do a project where readers send in thank-you letters? People love to tell stories as well as read them. You could run it over a number of weeks, then with permission from the letter writers, maybe interview some of them and make a big fanfare, keeping momentum going. And it would be something cheerful to share, rather than all this negative stuff in the press day after day.'

'*Somerley News* isn't like that, Gran. We try to share the good things for the most, but we do have to show both sides sometimes.'

'So this would be all nice and sweet.'

Grace went quiet, deep in thought.

'Thank-you letters could be a great project, Grace,' Eve replied. 'When I was younger, after birthdays and Christmases, I had to write them to everyone who bought me a gift. It took forever sometimes! But it was a lovely gesture, now I think about it. This could be something for the kids to reminiscence about with their parents and grandparents, too.'

'It would get all ages involved, talking about it and writing letters,' Rose added. 'You could even visit the schools and set up a project within a project. And it wouldn't take much to promote. I bet Tom would be happy with that.'

Grace sat upright, wide-eyed with excitement. 'Gran, I think you might be onto something here. I'm going to get my laptop and put down some thoughts.'

Eve reached across for her mum's hand and gave it a squeeze. 'Thanks for that. I haven't seen her smile like that in a long while.'

'I do have my talents.' Rose chuckled. 'Although I think they run in the family.'

'I bet you can't come up with a name for the project, too.'

'Pour me a little more of that mocktail, and I'll give it some thought.'

Eve grinned. Family gatherings were the best.

## CHAPTER SIX

Grace hid a yawn behind her hand. She'd barely had a wink of sleep after Rose had come up with the letter project, spending hours putting together a digital presentation for today's meeting. Afterwards, she'd been too wired to nod off.

She wondered how her idea would be perceived. Maybe she hadn't thought of everything just yet, but she was keen to hear everyone's thoughts and questions about it. Grace wasn't one to get down about constructive criticism. She liked input from others but, equally, this would be her baby. Grace would be the lead from start to finish.

She ran through her bullet list of things needing to be done if she got the green light. There would be promotional articles to write, spreadsheets to create as a way of recording the letters coming in, and also what had been printed in which edition of the *Somerley News*, as well as what was waiting to go to press the following week.

The added bonus could be articles coming from the results of the letters. There might be some feel-good stories that she could share. As long as the residents of Somerley were willing to write enough letters, this was doable.

'Morning.' Della walked across the office floor towards them. 'I come with treats.'

'A breakfast roll would be nice,' Joe said. 'Bacon and egg?'

'Funny, ha ha! Hasn't Fiona banned you from fry-ups?'

'What she doesn't know won't hurt her.' Joe raised his eyebrows. 'And I won't tell if you don't.'

'Nice try.' Della sat down at her desk and rummaged in her colossal handbag. She pulled out a brown paper bag. 'I've been to The Coffee Stop and brought some muffins and pastries, though, if one of them might do the trick instead.'

'I won't say no.' Joe leaned across his desk and took the bag from her. He delved inside for the first choice.

Grace had been checking over her notes and hadn't heard any of the conversation going on around her until Della prodded her on the arm and thrust a muffin in her face.

'White chocolate and raspberry,' she said. 'Your favourite.'

'Thanks, I'll have it after team meeting.' She smiled, wondering why Della was being so nice all of a sudden.

'Oh, yes, it's the big day. It'll be interesting to hear your thoughts, alongside sharing my own.'

Grace swallowed, instantly feeling the pressure she'd been trying to keep at bay.

Della laughed. 'Don't worry! You've done this kind of thing before.' She picked up her mug and went to the staffroom, not offering to make anyone else a drink while she was there.

'You have,' Joe soothed.

'Yes, but not on such a large scale. And to be fair, the only projects I've done was the teddy bear's picnic during the last school summer holidays and what's your favourite shoe.'

'You'll be fine, I'm sure. Heads-up, it's time to go.'

Grace saw Tom on his way towards the meeting room. She picked up her laptop, left her nerves behind, and followed Joe. Della came in a few moments after them.

Once everyone was settled, Tom went through the items on their agenda. 'Okay, let's have your ideas for the autumn community project,' he said finally. 'Joe, do you want to go first?'

While Grace listened to Joe, she wondered if her idea would pass muster. But he hadn't come up with much more than when she'd last spoken to him, and she thought maybe he'd done that purposely to give her a shot.

Della's project was good, though, involving photographs of years gone by and dressing up for school projects. Grace's heart sank with every new point she came up with. It was similar to her first thoughts around memories of Somerley but would involve more age groups. How on earth was she going to compete with that? She didn't want to be defeatist, but was her project strong enough?

'Grace, what have you got for us?' Tom asked next.

*You've got this.*

She took a deep breath, lifted the lid on her laptop, and turned it around to face the room. 'One Letter.'

She went over everything she'd popped onto slides, chatting points through when anyone stopped her for more details, and answering questions on further thoughts. At the end, she closed her laptop with a sense of relief.

Tom glanced at her. 'You've certainly given this some thought.'

'I have.' Grace hoped her skin wouldn't redden at her blatant lie. She had only developed it after her conversation with Rose the night before, so a few hours tops.

'I think it's a great idea,' Joe pointed out. 'It's far better than my effort.' He gave her a surreptitious wink.

'So do I,' Della remarked. 'It's not as good as mine but it will get papers bought.'

Grace ignored her jibe, sensing that Tom would most probably go with Della's idea.

Tom was deep in thought, rubbing at his chin.

Grace crossed her fingers beneath the table. She hadn't wanted anything this much since she was at school and had coveted the chocolate bar that was on offer each week if she got the most spellings right.

Tom sat for a moment longer, and then his eyes fell on Grace. 'Okay, let's give One Letter a go. I can find you some sponsors to bring in a little more cash if necessary for your prizes – not that you're going to need that much as costs will be low. That's a brilliant idea for that in itself.'

Grace couldn't believe her ears. He was going to go for Project One Letter!

'Really?' she asked, feeling like that five-year-old after approval again.

'Really,' Tom replied.

Grace beamed. This was a great chance to prove to Tom what she was capable of. Maybe this could get her the promotion to Joe's job when he retired.

'So, if you can pass your notes over to Della and she can dish out the jobs required. Grace, you and Joe can help out where necessary. Let's see what we can conjure up from the people of Somerley.'

'Oh, I thought you'd want me to...' Her words tailed off when she realised she'd been wrong to think she would be the lead officer. Tom had only wanted the idea. Della was always going to run the show.

Della smirked, a little unkindly, Grace thought. Joe winked at her, as if to say better luck next time. Tom had already gone.

Grace conjured up another smile. The first thing she did after she left the room was find a quiet spot to ring her mum.

'Hi, love. How did it go?'

'I got the go-ahead.'

'You did? Oh, that's wonderful news.' The line was quiet. 'I guess there's a but coming?'

'Tom loved my idea.'

'I knew he would.'

'I'm not leading, though. He gave it to Della. I thought this was my big chance, Mum.'

'Well, you'll just have to make such an excellent job of it that Tom will be so impressed and let you lead on the next one.'

'I suppose.' It wasn't fair that Grace hadn't got to run the project, but her mum was right. She would do whatever was necessary to succeed, even if it meant tackling things she'd rather not be doing.

# CHAPTER SEVEN

Eve went through to the living room, a bottle of wine lodged carefully under her arm, two glasses in one hand and a bowl of crisps in the other. She plonked them all on the coffee table and sat down next to her friend.

'Friday night in with Fiona,' she said with a dramatic sigh. 'I have been waiting for this all week.'

'Any particular reason?' Fiona sat forward to pour the wine. 'You're not in need of a pep talk, are you?'

'No, nothing like that. It's always good to see you. I look forward to our natters. How's Joe doing?'

'He's not losing much weight, so I assume he's getting his calories from elsewhere.' She rolled her eyes and then laughed. 'Sounds as if he's got another lover!'

'He's definitely got another love – food is the way to his heart – but I know he'd never be with anyone else. He only has eyes for you.'

Fiona and Joe had been friends with Eve and Clark since they'd met in their early twenties. Fiona worked at the chemist on the high street. A few years older than Eve at sixty-one, she wore her greying hair loose when out and about and tied in a ponytail at work. Bright-blue eyes shone behind tortoiseshell-framed glasses, a welcoming smile going with them for the most part.

They'd met one night in the Hope and Anchor. Clark and Eve had been in a group for the Thursday pub quiz. Fiona had bustled over to ask if she and Joe could join them, and they'd been a foursome ever since. They had so many fond memories to share that they never tired of reminiscing.

Eve relished their time together. Not only was Fiona a warm person, but she was a secret keeper, which was just as well as the tales she could tell about people's ailments would be a gossip fest.

Yet one of the reasons why Eve enjoyed her Friday hook-up with Fiona so much was because, without Joe being there, she didn't have to think that Clark was gone. It had been hard on the foursome to go down to three so suddenly and, even though her friends had always been there for her, their lives had changed, too.

She and Clark couldn't just pop round for an impromptu barbecue on a hot evening. Or arrange to go away for a week in the sun, as they'd often done through the years. They were always there for her, always would be, but a corner of their square was missing, and when she was with them both, it became too obvious.

'Joe was telling me about the project that Grace pitched today,' Fiona said. 'It sounds like a fun idea.'

'Yes, Rose gave her the initial seed, and Grace added her sparkle to it.' Eve took the glass of wine Fiona held out for her and reached for the crisps. She placed the bowl in the middle of the settee and popped a few in her mouth.

'I think Grace will sell it well,' Eve went on afterwards. 'She has such a flair for it, and people really take to her.'

'You and Clark did a wonderful job of raising her.'

'We did, didn't we?' Eve beamed, pulling her legs up to the side, being careful not to spill the crisps.

Grace had been a precious baby. After years of trying to conceive and then suffering four miscarriages, Eve had almost given up ever becoming a mum. But all that pain eased as soon as their daughter arrived.

She remembered seeing Clark's face light up with love when he'd first held Grace. He'd gazed into her eyes with so much adoration that Eve had welled up. All three of them had been blubbering wrecks for the first couple of days.

'So did you, with your girls,' Eve added. Fiona and Joe had three daughters, all married now with families of their own.

'We didn't do too badly.' Fiona chinked her glass with Eve's. 'Here's to the kids.'

'The kids.'

It was sad to think Clark would miss the birth of his grandchildren, if Grace, too, was blessed with a family, Eve thought. Whenever the subject came up, Grace said she'd like at least two. It was something to look forward to, although it would be a bittersweet moment.

And even if she was over the grief of losing him, Eve missed being part of a couple. As thoughts often did, they flipped one-eighty, and Mack popped into her mind. She decided to confide in Fiona.

'I met an old flame this week,' she said.

Fiona raised her eyebrows. 'Ooh, do tell.'

Eve filled her friend in on seeing Mack at work and how she knew him.

'And what is he like now?' Fiona was intrigued. 'Has age been kind?'

Eve tingled at the thought of how distinguished Mack was. His hands weren't all hard skin and weathered; hair thick enough to run fingers through. He had eyes that twinkled; lips that...

'You're blushing!'

'It's hot in here!' Eve waved away the comment.

'Well, I can't wait to meet him now.'

Eve laughed, and it morphed into a sigh. 'It's going to be weird, though, isn't it?'

'You'll adapt.' Fiona covered Eve's hand with her own. 'We just want to see you happy.'

'I know.'

'Why didn't you go with him to university?' Fiona queried. 'Or even to another one?'

'Oh, you know. My dad kept saying that I'd never amount to anything. That there was no point in me trying to get a degree as I was too dippy.'

'The bastard.'

'That's why me and Clark encouraged Grace to go to MMU, and then do a gap year before deciding what she wanted to do.' Eve shrugged. 'And then she ended up coming home.'

'Only because she saw the job at *Somerley News*. It was her degree that got her that. Along with her sparkling personality, of course.'

Eve glanced at the photo displayed proudly on the mantelpiece. It had been one of her proudest moments when Grace had graduated. She and Clark had gone suited and booted. Grace was radiant standing in the middle of them, she'd been so happy.

'But that stuff with your dad was nonsense, you do realise that now?' Fiona pouted. 'That man had a lot to answer for. He should have encouraged you to further your education, spreading your wings instead of clipping them. I reckon he was jealous.'

'Oh, it's water under the bridge now.'

'It's never too late to learn. What would you do now, if you had your time over?'

'I'm not sure, to be honest.'

'I think you're doing great as you are. It's not as if you're stuck behind the counter of the chemist like me.'

'Don't knock yourself. You are the fount of all medical knowledge!'

'Still, if I had my time again… It's never too late to do something new.' Fiona grinned. 'Business wise – or with the Macks of this world.'

'Baby steps, my friend,' Eve replied.

But she couldn't deny that the thought had crossed her mind once or twice with regards to a certain maintenance manager.

# CHAPTER EIGHT

Grace was in the office early the next morning. She often found she was able to get more done before too many of her work colleagues arrived. So far there was only her and Ethan in.

'Want a brew?' Ethan asked, yawning extremely loudly.

'I could murder one, thanks.'

'How's the project going? Do you need any stills?'

'Whatever you can throw my way. I'm just drafting out the feature. So, perhaps one of Somerley in its heyday. And...' She sighed. 'I don't know. Surprise me.'

He walked over to collect her mug. 'You've got this, Grace. Whatever happens, I'm sure you'll do a better job than Della.'

She grinned. 'Thanks for the vote of confidence.'

Grace had always liked Ethan. Another local lad, he was getting married later that year to his partner, Riley, who ran Chandler's Shoes on the high street. They made an attractive couple. Grace always teased them, saying they were the Posh and Becks of Somerley.

'I worked with her a few years ago, and she's very competitive,' Ethan continued. 'I was surprised to see Tom had hired her, to be fair.'

'Perhaps he wasn't privy to her antics.'

'My friend went out with her for a few months. She was very controlling.'

'Oh?' It wasn't like Ethan to gossip, so she pointed to the seat.

He sat down across from her. 'He stopped coming out with us for a while. Said he was loved-up and preferred to stay in with Della. He'd been such a laugh, but I think she wore him down. And when he finally saw sense and finished things with her, boy, did she go a bit over the top.'

'Doing what?'

'Sending him emails, bombarding his phone with messages. Then leaving notes on his car. At one point he said he'd go to the police and say she was harassing him.'

'Sounds like she was.'

Ethan nodded. 'She stopped once he said that to her. Shortly afterwards, she left. I hadn't realised she was still in Somerley until she turned up here.'

'Well, thank goodness it's only temporary.'

'Hopefully.'

He stood up to go, but Grace sensed he wanted to add something more.

'Let's say she's not averse in using underhand tactics to get her own way,' he said. 'Just be careful.'

'I will.'

Grace sat silent for a moment as he walked away. Then she went back to reading through what she had written so far, not giving his words any extra thought.

*Do you have a happy memory to share?*

Somerley News *are looking for feel-good stories for a competition that will be run over the next eight weeks. The project was the idea of Grace Warrington, feature assistant, and was inspired by her nan, Rose.*

*'I was asked to come up with something that we could involve the public in,' Grace said. 'We were chatting over dinner, my mum, too, and my gran mentioned writing letters. She said that the world was full of negativity right now, so wouldn't it be lovely if the people of Somerley wrote about things that made them happy? Project One Letter was created.'*

*We are asking you to write a thank-you letter to someone who has done something special for you, changed your life, or has been genuinely kind. It can be as short or as long as you like, and we will be printing several of them in our newspaper every week. Some of them will be displayed at the local library and in places around the town. They can be anonymous, or you can include names as long as you've asked the person you're writing about.*

*There are also prizes to be won. For further details, check out the list below for the type of things we are after. But remember, these are your memories. So anything too personal that you don't want to share, you won't be able to send. Full details can also be found on our website.*

Satisfied with her initial thoughts, Grace saved the document and closed it for now. It was okay for a draft, and she would come back to it in the morning. It was going out in this week's edition, so she had a day to get it right, and she couldn't be more excited.

She wondered what she would write about if she were to take part. Obviously with there being an overall prize, she couldn't include her own letter, but even so, she'd have to think of something to say. Someone was bound to ask her what she would write about, and she wanted to be ready with a witty anecdote or two to come back with.

What would she include? A thought popped into her head of her granddad and her dad in the garden the summer before they'd died. They were both trying to be in charge of the barbecue. She, her mum, and gran were stifling laughter as they watched.

Dad was flipping burgers, and Granddad was telling him to be quicker as they were burning.

Dad said that burning added to the flavour. Granddad replied to say he'd never heard such nonsense. He hadn't realised it was a joke and that Dad was winding him up.

Later, they'd sat in the garden, eating and chatting, and it had been a lovely afternoon. The competitiveness had gone once the food had been cooked.

She'd give anything to be able to thank them for what they'd done for her until they'd died. She missed them so much.

With Grace living at home again, she and her mum reminisced a lot about her dad. It was nice to see Eve could do that without getting too upset now. It was different when it came to Granddad, though. Neither Mum nor her gran talked much about him. Of course, she knew they hadn't forgotten him either, but it was always her dad brought up in conversation.

Her gran had been a beautiful woman when she was younger, and if Grace aged half as well, she would be pleased. Rose always dressed immaculately and was well groomed. Grace liked that about her. She made an effort, no matter what. Like her mum, Grace had inherited Rose's small build, dark hair, and clear skin. Gran had far less wrinkles than her friend, Iris, too.

Her mind went back to the task in hand. She assumed

she'd have lots of letters about parties, birthdays, weddings, holidays. She only hoped her friends and neighbours, and the people who stopped her on the streets of Somerley on a regular basis, would join in the fun. If they didn't, there would be empty pages she'd need to fill each week.

# CHAPTER NINE

Eve had run a few errands and was on her way to Rose's flat when she spotted Mack waving to get her attention.

'Hi, Eve.' He came up beside her. 'Have you been, gone, and come back today, or have you not left yet?'

'I had to nip to the chemist for Mum while she waits in for a parcel, although I have to say she's more in than out if she's not expecting anything.' She raised her hand to indicate the bag she was carrying. 'Thank goodness for mobile phones. When my dad was alive, Mum had been practically housebound. Now with her own wheels and a friend who she goes out with regularly, there's often no finding her at home. At least with the phone, I can check her whereabouts.' Eve stopped, realising she was rambling.

'It's such a lovely day, and I don't feel like a sandwich on my own in the garden.' Mack threw a thumb over his shoulder, to where the roof of the local pub could be seen above the hedge. 'Would you like to grab a spot of lunch with me?'

'Today?' Eve was taken aback by his offer, which must clearly have shown on her face as Mack's smile dropped.

'Well, if you're busy, we could do it—'

'No, I'm free, and yes, that would be nice.'

'Oh!' The smile was back.

'You sound as if you expected me to say no.'

A blush spread over his cheeks. 'I did, actually.'

Eve laughed. 'Any reason why I should have?'

'No!' He laughed, too. 'Not at all.'

'So... what time is your break?'

'Twelve.'

'Great. I'll meet you by the back gate. You have found that?'

Mack nodded. 'It must be wonderful not to stagger home the long way.'

'I'll see you at twelve then.' Eve checked her watch. Only an hour to go.

For the first time in a long while, Eve had a spring in her step. Not that she was going to tell her mum why that was. It was only a bite to eat Mack had invited her along to. Still, there was a ball of excitement starting in her stomach at the thought.

Just before midday, she went into the bathroom to freshen up. The weather had left her with a glow to her skin, and a tan always made her feel better. She applied fresh lipstick and a dash of mascara. Then she sprayed her perfume liberally.

'Where are you off to now?' Rose eyed her suspiciously.

'Mack and I are having a bite to eat across at the pub.'

'Ooh, have a wonderful time.' Rose smirked, a knowing look on her face.

Eve disappeared pretty sharpish before she got the third degree. It *was* only lunch with Mack, but she knew her mum was already seeing further into it. After all, wasn't that what she wanted it to be?

Mack was waiting for her as planned, and she waved when he spotted her.

'I'm famished,' he said. 'This warm weather is giving me an appetite.'

They walked to the pub, chatting amicably about anything and everything to do with Somerley Heights. Eve was amazed how comfortable she felt with him already. It was as if the years they hadn't seen each other had evaporated.

The pub was a rustic affair, low wooden beams and red dralon seat coverings and curtains. A mighty collection of beer mats from around the world adorned one wall above the bench seating, and there was an inglenook fireplace for colder days.

The area they ordered food in was practically empty as most people were enjoying the warm weather. An elderly man sat with his dog at his feet reading a newspaper. Eve smiled when he caught her eye.

Once served, they took their drinks out to the beer garden, eyes adjusting from the gloom to the brightness again. Over in the far corner, there was an empty table in the shade. Eve pointed to it.

'Quick, let's nab that.'

They settled in their seats, across from one another.

'Have you been here before?' she asked. 'It's a lovely place, and their meals are legendary.'

'No, first time.' Mack took a large gulp of his drink. 'Ah, I needed that.'

'Do you have a lot planned for this afternoon?'

'Just overseeing contractors. Sometimes they give me headaches, but so far so good today. How about you?'

'Well, as you know, I work three hours each morning, but I also have a part-time sewing business, and I have a couple of jobs booked in. I'm lucky that I don't have to work for someone full-time.'

Eve looked away then, feeling embarrassed about her situation. She knew she was lucky, but she didn't like sharing details with people. But then, this was Mack. She didn't need to hide anything.

'When my husband, Clark, died, we had policies that paid out. There wasn't much left to pay on the mortgage, and it left me with a bit of a safety net to fall back on. How long have you been back in Somerley?'

'A few weeks. I'm contracted for twelve months, so I'm not sure after that. I was into financial management before. It was quite stressful at times, so I fancied a change.'

Eve suspected there was a story in there that Mack didn't want to share. Perhaps he would feel up to it another time.

She hoped there would be one.

'I never quite cracked something I enjoyed career wise, despite going to university,' Mack went on.

It was as if a shockwave went through her body, almost transporting her to a time when she hadn't wanted him to leave. It had been the end for them when he'd set off to Lancashire, leaving her behind in Somerley.

'What about you?' he asked, when she was quiet.

Eve smiled, blushing a little. He could obviously sense her discomfort so had changed the subject.

'I was a shop supervisor until Grace was born. She didn't come along until I was twenty-eight. We'd been trying for a baby for a while, and I was beginning to think I might never carry one full term, so when I stayed pregnant, I quit my job.'

'Can I see a photo of her?'

Eve took out her phone, scrolling through her images until she found one of them both. She handed Mack the phone.

'Wow, she's the spit of you,' he exclaimed. 'You must be so proud.'

'I am. She keeps me sane, too. She's great company.'

'I'd love to meet her, if she's anything like her mum.'

Mack was still looking at the photo, almost as if he'd said

what he was thinking. He glanced up at her then, grinning as he gave the phone back to her.

'What about you?' she queried. 'Children, grandchildren?'

'Two boys and a girl. Four grandkids so far, three boys and a girl.'

It was Mack's turn to show off with photos.

Eve sat across from him, warmed by his closeness, and wondering if he ever regretted leaving her behind. She glanced up to see him staring at her and she wriggled in her seat, her cheeks hotting up again.

Luckily, their sandwiches arrived, and there was no time to chat intensely after that. Mack didn't have long before he was due back at work.

Later, when they'd returned to Somerley Heights, Grace stopped once she drew level with her car.

'That was nice. Thanks for paying for lunch,' she said. 'My shout next time?'

'I'm already looking forward to it.' Mack leaned close to kiss her on the cheek. 'I'll see you tomorrow.'

'You will.' She breathed in musky aftershave before he moved away again. A smile played on her lips.

That evening, when she was watching TV, she couldn't stop thinking about him. Their hour together had been pleasant, conversation easy and, even so, she was keen to learn more about him.

She wondered if now might be their time to pick up from where they'd left things. Did they have unfinished business to attend to?

# CHAPTER TEN

Like clockwork every Thursday morning, Rose and her friend, Iris, visited The Coffee Stop. They'd known both of the previous proprietors, Lily and Bernard, well and were always sad to think of them gone. But their memories lived on in the two new owners, Chloe and Kate, who had turned the old run-down Lil's Pantry into a fine establishment serving artisan cakes and bespoke coffees among the usual wares.

This morning, the two friends hadn't long sat down when Livvy, who worked in the adjoining book shop, came through to them. She had a book in her hand and held it up as she got to the table.

'Just in, ladies,' she said. 'I saved you a copy.'

Rose and Iris gasped in delight. Scarlett Helton was one of their favourite authors, and her new book wasn't out until tomorrow.

'You are a treasure.' Rose wrapped her hands around it greedily. 'Can I go first, Iris? I'm dying to know what happened to Meryl and Hugh since the last book in the series.'

'I suppose.' Iris tutted in a friendly manner. 'I'm halfway through a Carole Matthews's book at the moment anyway.'

'We can do a swap then.' Rose reached her purse from her bag, took out a note, and passed it to Livvy. 'Thank you, darling. What would we do without you? How're things?'

'Oh, you know. Just keeping busy. Business is brisk.'

'And how's your lovely daughter, Pip? And your sister, Hannah, and the delectable Doug?'

'They're fine, thanks.' Livvy laughed, fidgeting with her dark-brown ponytail. 'Pip is growing extremely lanky. She towers over me.'

'And the delightful Callan?' Rose leaned forward to whisper. 'Is he still on the scene, and are you madly in love?'

'Yes, and yes!' Livvy spotted someone going through to the book shop. 'I'd better be off. I'll be back with your change once I've rung your order through the till.'

'Oh, never mind about that. Put it to use buying sweets to share with the little ones.'

Rose watched Livvy leave, glad to see that she was happy now. Livvy had been away from Somerley for twenty years before coming back and reconciling with her sister, Hannah.

'How did your project idea go down?' Iris stirred her cappuccino and brought it to her lips.

'It was a success!' Rose had been delighted when Grace had rung to tell her she'd been given the go-ahead. 'There's going to be an award's presentation, too. We'll both be invited, I'm sure. It will be a nice evening out.'

'Another one.' Iris rolled her eyes, and they laughed.

Rose and Iris had known each other since they were twelve, worked together, raised family's side by side, and shared life's ups and downs. In their later years, they spent more time out of their homes than in them and were often called the troublesome twins as they were so alike. Both had the same build, not frail, mind. Iris's silver-grey hair was cut in a short flattering style to Rose's elegant bob, but they each had bright eyes. Embracing life together every day suited them.

A young man in navy-blue overalls opened the door, a list in his hand. He wiped muddy boots on the welcome mat before joining the queue at the counter.

Rose shuddered as a memory rushed to the front of her mind. She put down her drink.

'Rose, are you all right?' Iris asked, concern in her voice.

*Rose was cleaning the mud from Harry's shoes ready to polish them when she heard the front door open and then close with a slam.*

*'Is that you, love?' she shouted.*

*'Who else would it be?' He tutted, coming through. He took one look at the newspaper on the table, the shoes and the polish with the rags. 'Why haven't you done those before I got home?'*

*'I didn't see them until I got in from work.'*

*'But I told you last night that they needed cleaning.'*

*'Did you?' Rose frowned, certain he hadn't.*

*'I said I wanted them done so I could go out in them this evening.'*

*'But I thought we were going to stay in together. I have a stew cooking.'*

*Harry's fist banged on the table, making her jump and the tin of polish bounce off it. 'You never listen to a word I say, do you? I said I was going out.'*

*Rose said nothing this time. He hadn't told her, but it wasn't worth saying that. He would get into a worse mood, and she'd rather have the peace and quiet when he left the house again. Instead, she put on a smile.*

*'Of course you did,' she lied. 'And I wish I'd finished these shoes in time. They won't take me long now. Why don't you pop upstairs for a wash and change, and they'll be shining by the time you come downstairs?'*

*He left the room, muttering about how useless she was. Rose was determined not to be like Harry's mother, and yet look at her. For now, she'd settle with easing him into doing things her way. She wouldn't let him push her around forever.*

'Rose!' Iris reached across the table to touch her arm.

'Hmm?' Rose came back into the room, a weak smile all she could muster. 'Sorry, I was miles away there for a moment.'

'I said, are you all right? You've gone ever so pale.'

It was often the slightest thing that jolted her back to unhappy times. A whiff of aftershave, a man with the same build as Harry, or like today, a muddy boot.

'Yes, I'm fine. Would you like another drink? My treat? Eve is popping over, but I have another half an hour.'

'Marvellous.'

Rose bustled off to the counter to place an order. Seeing the man with the boots in front of her, it distressed her to see how even the tiniest of connections to a memory could still affect her, even after three years without Harry.

She wished it didn't, but she wasn't sure the feelings would ever leave her. More was the pity.

Rose was back at home now after a wonderful morning with Iris. Eve was folding washing out of the dryer, ready to put away for her.

'How are you getting on with the delightful maintenance manager?' Rose asked.

'He's really nice, Mum. It's great fun catching up on old times, filling each other in with what's happened throughout the years. He wants to walk around Somerley with me so I can show him what's changed.' Eve smiled. 'Or rather what hasn't. I like that about Somerley, though, don't you? It's still so familiar and full of charm.'

'That's not what you used to say when you and Mack were an item. I remember you kids were bored because there was nothing to do.'

'There wasn't!'

'I know. But you're right, it does have its moments. Personally, I think he just wants to kiss you behind the bike sheds again.'

'Mum!'

'You're blushing.'

'I am not.' Eve laughed.

'I had a first love, before I met your father.'

Eve's mouth dropped open. 'I never knew that.'

'I never told anyone. His name was Cedric. Things might have been different if he'd stayed around, but it wasn't meant to be. One minute he was working in the factory and the next he was gone, so our relationship was over before it had even begun. We shared a kiss, and that was that.'

'Oh, Mum, that's so sad. Was this before you met Dad?'

Rose shook her head. 'It was when I was dating him.'

Eve frowned.

'Don't seem so surprised. It does happen. Your dad and I had only been courting for a few weeks. It wasn't as if we were going steady at that point.' Her eyes sparkled with a mischievous glint. 'I would see Cedric in the works canteen, and we started smiling at each other. Then he spoke to me, and then a bit more and, by the end of the first fortnight, I was waiting for break time in anticipation of seeing him. He used to make me laugh so much.'

Rose's face clouded over then. 'One Friday, he asked me out on a date. I said yes but I told him I would need to speak to your dad first. I thought it was fair that I explained to him what was happening. That weekend, I was too nervous to pluck up the courage. And when I got to work on Monday, Cedric wasn't there.'

'You were going to break up with Dad for Cedric?'

Rose nodded. 'When I asked around, it seemed there had been some trouble and he'd left in a hurry.'

'Did you ever find out why?'

'No, and my heart was broken. I didn't know what to think.' Rose hung her head, unable to look her daughter in the eye. 'It was your dad who insisted I forget him. And we all know how that ended, don't we?'

## CHAPTER ELEVEN

'Paper is in.' Joe slapped a copy down on Grace's desk.

Grace grabbed for it, her stomach in knots. Her article would be in it and, even though she'd seen the layout digitally, she wanted to view it as a reader would. She opened it to page four, where she knew the two-page spread would sit.

Only to see a photograph of Della perched on the end of her desk, holding up a blank white envelope. She groaned. Ethan had taken a similar photo of her. Della must have swapped it out at the last minute.

'She's taking credit for my idea, Joe.' Grace showed him the piece. 'It's not fair.'

'And you'll rise above it. She won't be here for long.'

'You think? She's after your job.'

Joe sniggered. 'The chances of her getting that are extremely low.'

Grace was all ears. 'How do you know?'

'Just a theory.'

Grace got back to reading the article. *Can You Share the Best Day of Your Life?* the headline, she realised Della must have also changed, read. So her original idea for thank-you letters had changed, too. She wished someone would have consulted her about it first.

'What do you think?' she asked regardless, looking for Joe's approval.

'It reads great. You've made it appealing to all age groups.'

She beamed. 'I have, haven't I?' She reached for her phone, took a few snaps of the spread, and was about to send it to Liam when she stopped.

Old habits die slowly, she sighed, upset because she couldn't share it with anyone. Liam had never shown much interest in her job unless it was testing out freebies or getting complimentary dinners at new restaurants. Something the two of them could take advantage of so that it didn't involve being with other people.

She sent them to her mum and gran instead.

Tom came over to congratulate her. 'It looks really good, Grace. I'm sure you'll have lots of letters arriving soon.'

'I have my system ready to record them all.' She opened the colour-coded spreadsheet she'd created.

'So all we do now is sit and wait for the letters to come in,' Joe said.

'And hold pages four and five for the next three months!' Grace grinned.

'Great.' Tom nodded. 'Ask Della to pop in to see me when she arrives, will you?'

'Will do.'

'Hope she gets pulled over the coals for her punctuality,' Joe muttered once Tom was back in his office. 'She's never here on time.'

'You've noticed that, too? She does come up with some slick excuses, though.' Grace sniggered. 'Researching articles, my arse.'

Grace dived back into her work. She couldn't wait to see what post came in tomorrow. What would the first letter be about?

Her project would be a huge success. It didn't matter who took credit for managing it. It was going to be great, regardless.

Half an hour later, after fetching the post, Grace arrived back in time to see Della storm out of Tom's office and back to her desk.

Della pouted. 'Have either of you said anything to Tom about me?' she questioned, hostility in her voice. 'Because I've just got a roasting for coming in late.'

'If you want to stay longer than covering Kim's maternity leave,' Joe said, 'then I suggest you get here on time. Tom hates tardiness.'

'It's been a handful of times at the most,' she whined.

Joe shrugged. 'Just saying. We've worked here for years. We know what he prefers.'

'Yeah, well, I'm my own woman. I don't like being told what to do, especially over petty things like timekeeping.'

Grace was going to speak out in Tom's defence, but seeing Joe shaking his head, she refrained again.


In the town centre, Eve parked on the high street and rushed into Somerley Stores. One of the proprietors, Ellen Savage, was behind the till and waved as she saw her. The small queue was gone by the time Eve had filled her basket with what she needed.

'There's a new guy in town,' Eve said to her as she popped it on the counter.

'Oh?'

'Yes, he's the new maintenance manager at Somerley Heights?'

'You're a bit behind the times.'

'I haven't seen you since last week or else I would have said something then.'

Eve smirked. 'How do you know about him already?'

'I find out everything in here.' Ellen took the bag Eve offered and filled it up as she rang goods through the till. 'He came in for some groceries yesterday. He's rented a flat in Helen Street, on his own.'

'You don't hang around much.' Eve was impressed.

'I make it my job to ask.' Ellen tapped the side of her nose twice. 'Besides, I did it for you. That's nineteen pounds, forty-five, altogether.'

'*Me?*' Eve frowned, pressing her card to the reader.

'He seems your type.'

'He was many moons ago.'

That had Ellen flummoxed.

Eve grinned and put the card back in her purse. 'We used to be a thing in high school.'

'Oh, first loves! Maybe this will be a second chance romance.' Ellen stopped. 'Or maybe your Grace could have a sugar daddy!'

'Ugh, I hope not. He's old enough to be her father.'

Ellen held her hand out for money from the next customer who only wanted a newspaper. 'Thanks, love.' She turned back to Ellen once he'd gone. 'Is he the same age as you?'

Eve nodded, picking up her shopping. 'But he left Somerley when he was eighteen. I hadn't seen him since then.'

'Sounds like you have a story to tell.'

Eve laughed and shook her head. 'Nothing sordid.'

'Well, I thought he was a dish.' Ellen raised her eyebrows. 'Your turn to find out more.'

'I'll let you know,' Eve fibbed because she wasn't one to spread gossip.

Nevertheless, she was intrigued about Mack's return. Thirty years was a long time to be away from Somerley.

# 1973

*My dearest Rose,*

*It's my thirtieth birthday! Whenever I reach a milestone, I think of you more. I wonder if you're happy but know I will never try to find out. Our lives are separate, but still, it doesn't stop me thinking of you. Wondering how you are. Hoping that you're happy.*

*I'm married now, to Betty. She's one of five sisters – five, can you imagine? She's the middle sister, and I quite like that. The two older ones are bossy, and the two younger ones keep me sane.*

*Betty and I had a lovely wedding. We met when I was twenty-two, got married a year later, and then Michael came along shortly afterwards. I have two children now. Michael is six, and Rachel is four. They are both really bright. They must get that from their mother, because it certainly isn't from me!*

*I think you would like Betty. She is such a light in my life. She was a nurse when we met and has taken time out to look after the family. Once the children are older, she will go back to it, I'm sure. She misses it, even though she says there is no better job than being a mum.*

*I wonder how many children you have now, Rose? I'm not sure if we want to have anymore, but you never know. We have one of each, that's enough. But as I was an only child, I feel the need to have a large family.*

*We bought a terraced cottage, on the outskirts of Hexham. It needs a lot of work doing on it. Last year we had a new kitchen fitted, and we're saving to do the bathroom next.*

*We also took our first holiday abroad! I can tell you I was terrified as we took off from the airport, holding on to the arms of the chair for dear life. But, once we were in the air, I relaxed, and although I wouldn't say I enjoyed flying, it's nice to get the sand, sea, and sun at the other end.*

*We went to Majorca. What a wonderful place, and so hot. We all enjoyed it very much and hope to go overseas each summer.*

*I hope you are keeping well.*

*All my love,*

*Cedric*

## CHAPTER TWELVE

At work the next morning, Grace was desperate for the post to arrive. It usually came around half past nine and, even though she wasn't expecting many letters yet, she couldn't wait to read the first one. Hopefully there might be a hundred or so in total over the coming weeks.

When she got a call from Flora, she eagerly dashed into the reception area.

'Hey.' She jumped to a halt behind the desk. 'Let me at it, then.'

'It's all yours.' Flora handed it to her. 'There's a ton of the stuff.'

Grace flicked through it all, but there was nothing addressed to her except two circulars she received every month.

'Oh, that's disappointing,' she said, her shoulders drooping.

'The article only went out last night,' Flora soothed. 'Give it time.'

'I was expecting at least one letter today, though. I

thought someone might be interested enough to write straightaway.'

'Maybe so, but even if someone had written and then posted one last night, it wouldn't be picked up by the postie until today. So the earliest you'll get something is tomorrow.'

'I knew that.' Grace grinned, realising she hadn't even given that a thought. 'Although someone could have hand-delivered one.'

Flora smirked. 'Stop being an eager beaver.'

Grace flounced off after giving her a mock-evil stare. Of course there would be nothing today for the reason Flora had stated.

But half an hour later, there was another call from Flora.

'You have a visitor,' she said. 'Mr Postman is asking for you.'

Grace raced across to reception again, smiling when she looked up into a tanned face with deep-blue eyes below short brown hair.

'Tyler!' she cried. 'Are you back on our route?' Tyler had gone to Grace's school and, although he was three years older than her, they'd been friends since well into their teens. He lived in a flat behind Somerley church.

'Yes, they've changed our rotas again.' Tyler rolled his eyes.

'Do you have anything for little old me?'

He held up a white envelope. 'It's addressed to you, but there's no stamp. I didn't have the heart to take it back to the depot after reading your article last night, but don't tell anyone or else I'll get the sack.'

'You already have the sack.' Grace pointed to his post bag. 'Sack, geddit?'

Tyler groaned. 'I see we still share the same sense of humour. How are you doing?'

'I'm okay, thanks.'

'Still in love?'

'Nope, that's all over.'

Tyler's shoulders lifted for a slight second before falling again. 'Oh, I'm sorry to hear that.'

'It was a relief, really. How are things with you?'

'Fine, still single and fancy free.' He raised his eyebrows in comical fashion. 'I'm a babe magnet, but that one long-term relationship keeps alluding me.'

'I wonder why,' she teased. 'Is it because you can't dance for toffee?'

'That's a bit harsh. I only stood on your toes a few times.'

'Well, perhaps it's because of your poor taste in music.'

'I happen to like lots of the modern stuff, too!'

'You sound as if you're in your seventies.'

'I feel like it some days. My legs ain't what they used to be.' He pointed at the envelope. 'Aren't you going to open that?'

'Yes, in private.'

'But it's only fair that I see the first letter after I put myself in so much jeopardy to get it to you.'

'It might be rubbish, someone telling me it's a stupid idea. Or a poison pen letter.'

'To you?' He shook his head. 'I don't think you've ever upset anyone in your life.'

'You'd be surprised working here. Some of the emails and messages I get after covering some stories are particularly nasty.'

'Really? I can't believe that.' He puffed out his chest. 'If you ever need a bodyguard...'

'I'd be sure to hire someone who could do the job,' she joked.

He snatched the letter from her hand. 'Ah, well, if you're going to be like that.'

'Give it to me, Tyler!' She reached up for it as he held it above his head. 'Ah, come on.'

He laughed, then handed it back to her. 'Open it now. I want to see what it says.'

Grace sighed: he wasn't going to give up. She pointed to the seating area. 'Okay then. But I want to read it myself first.'

They sat across from each other, and with an excited squeak, she opened the envelope. Inside was a handwritten note on lined paper.

*The best day of my life was when our doggie came to live with us. My daddy works very hard, and sometimes he does not get home in time for me to see him until the next day. I miss my daddy, but my mummy is the best. She looks after me so well.*

*One weekend, Mummy and Daddy told me to come into the kitchen as they had a surprise for me. I ran in, and there was a puppy on the floor! We named him Milo, and he's a cockapoo. I laughed very much at that.*

*There was pee and poo everywhere when Milo was little. And he kept chewing things and stealing everyone's socks. But now he is older, he is much better behaved.*

*Milo follows me everywhere. When I get home from school, he jumps all over me. He waggles his bottom so much that I think his tail is going to come off. He sits with me when I do my homework and when I'm watching TV.*

*He likes tennis balls very much.*

*Milo is one year old today. He is having a birthday cake and presents. We are having a tea party. My daddy says he will be home in time to celebrate. I'm looking forward to that.*

*Petra, aged 5 and 3/4*

. . .

'Oh, that's so sweet.' Grace passed the note to Tyler, waiting while he read it. 'I think she had a little help from someone to write it.'

'I wonder who her parents are. You might know them.'

'The odds of that around here are pretty much in my favour.'

'Not everyone in Somerley knows everyone else.'

'I know that, but it is a close-knit community – for the most part. Look at what happened when the community centre was threatened with closure.'

Grace hadn't long moved to features when the council had said they were closing the community centre. There had been uproar after their article had gone out about it. An opposition group had been created, raising funds, but it hadn't been enough. Luckily, local businessman, Robin Marriott, had stepped in and bought it. He'd renovated it, and now it was used most days and evenings.

'Are there any contact details?' Grace reached across for it and checked on the back. 'Oh, yes. I can contact Petra's family and do an article with her permission.' She clutched the letter to her chest. 'The first letter, and it's a lovely one.'

## CHAPTER THIRTEEN

Eve closed the door to Rose's flat and came out onto the communal corridor. She smiled seeing Mack ahead of her. He was up a ladder, changing a bulb.

'Hey.' His face lit up when he saw her approaching.

'Hi, Mack.' She couldn't help but smile. He really was a sight for sore eyes.

'Hey, how are you?' He stepped down until he was eye level with her.

The attraction Eve felt was instant. She wanted to reach out and touch him, and yet she didn't dare. But he made her feel good – surely that spoke volumes? She should be embracing life, not pushing it away.

'I'm well, thanks.' Eve decided to be brave for a change, because she did want to spend time getting to know Mack again. 'I was wondering if you'd like to come to mine for a meal one evening. We could have a proper catch-up. Obviously, if you're busy it's fine. I just—'

'I would love that.' He smiled. 'When are you free?'

'How about tomorrow?'

'Looking forward to it.'

He nodded, and she gave him her address.

'Does Maxine Flint still live in that street?'

'Her parents do. She left years ago. I can't remember the last time I saw her. She was married with a couple of kids.'

'Is she still in Somerley?'

'Why do you ask?'

'Just making conversation. You're not jealous, are you?'

She slapped his arm in a playful manner. 'I'm nothing of the sort! Now, is there anything you don't eat?'

'Seafood is not my thing. Other than that, I'm not fussy.'

'I'll see what I can rustle up. Half six do you?'

'Perfect.'

They said their goodbyes, and Eve dashed out to her car, all the while making a mental list of what she needed to buy.

She was pleased she'd spotted Mack now.

Grace was going to be on the local radio in a few minutes so went through to a side room for a bit of privacy. It was more to do with Della's prying eyes, because if she found out what was going on, she'd want to do the interview instead. Grace wanted the opportunity to shine this time.

Grace was great with talking to people, but doing anything live brought her out in a panic. She preferred to do interviews face to face. When she spoke down the telephone line, with no eye contact from anyone, her mind wandered from the original question, and she often just stuttered along. At least this time, she'd prepared a list of questions that she might be asked.

Her phone rang. 'Hi, Ray. How are you?'

'Not too bad, thanks. So, you're hoping to get some publicity? It will cost you.'

'I hear you're partial to the new range of doughnuts from the indoor market?'

Ray roared with laughter. 'Definitely the way to win a man over. I'll leave you hanging for five, while this track finishes, and then I'll be straight to you. Okay?'

'Okay!' Her voice sounded much more enthusiastic than she felt. While she listened to George Michael telling everyone to go outside, she took a few deep breaths. "Nothing is too big a mountain to climb when you're standing up and smiling," her dad used to say.

Grace got to her feet as the song ended, seconds before she was put live on air.

Three minutes later, she had pitched Project Best Day of Your Life and even persuaded Ray to send in a letter. Not that she thought he would, but it was nice of him to join in.

'All done,' Ray announced off air, music playing in the background again. 'I wish you well. The town could do with some nice things to talk about, the years we've just got through.'

'Indeed. Thanks a million for having me on your show again.'

'No worries. Come back on any time over the next few weeks until it's finished.'

'I will.'

'My favourite doughnut is anything with vanilla custard.'

She laughed as she said her goodbyes. All she hoped was that with the extra bit of publicity, plus the new article that would be read by people later that week, some letters should start to come in.

When she got back to her desk, Flora pointed to a few envelopes. 'Tada! These are for you!'

Grace reached for them greedily, spreading them out to count them. 'Only three? It's a start, I suppose.'

'And the more you write about individual letters in each week's edition, the more you'll have coming in.' Flora flicked her red hair out of her eyes. 'You should get us all to do our own best day letters until then. That could be a huge spread, and people would get to know us, too.'

'That's a great idea.' Grace didn't tell her she'd already thought about it. 'I doubt everyone would join in, though.'

'It doesn't have to be anything adventurous. We'd only need to do a hundred words each and you'd have a great feature.'

'Maybe we could link it to some of the businesses around here, give them a bit of free promo.'

'You see?' Flora grinned. 'You're all over this.'

Eve was hand sewing some missing sequins onto a ball gown when Grace came home that evening.

'Hi, love.' She smiled. 'Kettle hasn't long boiled if you want a brew.'

'I'll make us both one in a minute.' Grace sat down beside her on the settee. 'Watching anything interesting?'

'The usual. I heard you on the radio. You were great.'

'Thanks. I felt nervous before I went on, but it was okay. You seemed miles away when I came in.'

'I was thinking of you. I've asked Mack round for tea. I hope you don't mind.'

'Mack the maintenance manager from Somerley Heights?'

'The very same.'

'It's fine by me. You don't need my permission. I've been telling you to find a new man for ages.'

Eve grinned. 'I know you have, but I wasn't ready.'

'I wouldn't think anything of it, you know, if you're really keen on him.'

'Well, that's good because I'm hoping it might lead to a proper date.'

'That will be a proper date.'

'You know what I mean.'

'I do, and I'm pleased for you.'

'You're not sad about it?'

'Mum, you've been on your own for three years.'

'I know, but it's hard to move on after… but I am ready to start again.' She got up. 'Let's have a drink while we chat.'

Coffee made, giving her time to gather her thoughts, Eve rejoined Grace, handing a mug to her. 'I feel like I'm betraying your dad seeing Mack, but equally know I need to have fun, too.'

'Dad would never think like that. He'd want you to go out and make new memories with someone else.' Grace paused. 'What's he like, Mack?'

'Pretty nice-looking, I must say.' Eve got a photo up on her phone. She'd snapped it when Mack had been wrestling with one of the trees at work. She showed it to her now.

'Nice,' Grace agreed. 'But what I meant is what he's like as a person?'

'He's kind, thoughtful, and just like I remember him from when we were sixteen.'

'What does Gran think of him?'

'He's passed muster. He did when he was younger, too.' Eve enlightened Grace about old times.

'How exciting. This could be a second chance for you both. When can I meet him?'

'Whenever you want. I know he'd like that.'

They grinned at each other, and Eve was so pleased she'd raised a daughter who she could talk to like this.

'I'm glad you're okay with it, Grace.'

'As long as he treats you well, it's fine by me.'

Eve relaxed a little then. Of course, she would do what

she thought was right for herself, but it was important to her that her family were onside, too.

Because Mack had made her realise that even if it was tough to lose someone, it was even harder to miss out on what could have been.

## CHAPTER FOURTEEN

Della was at home that morning, finishing her makeup in the bathroom. Her mum appeared in the doorway, a pensive look on her face.

'What is it?' Della asked, worried by her expression.

'I can't find my watch.' Marianne rubbed at her wrist, where it would usually be. 'I think Chris stole it when he came round on Sunday.'

'Chris wasn't here at the weekend.' Della popped the mascara wand back in its tube. 'Hang on a minute, and I'll come and search for it with you.'

'I'm telling you, it's not here,' Marianne snapped. 'When I see him, I'm going to swing for him. He has no right to take my things.'

Della stared at herself in the mirror, hoping this latest episode wasn't going to blow up. Why was it always when she was getting ready for work?

'You'll have to tell him, Della,' Marianne went on. 'If he doesn't bring it back, I'm calling the police.'

'You don't have to do that, Mum!'

Della recalled a few days ago, when Marianne *had* called

the emergency services, telling the operator that Chris was about to stab her when her brother wasn't even in the country. Chris and his family were in Spain for a fortnight and didn't come back until the weekend. At least then, he might be able to calm Mum down. He was much better at it than her. Having said that, lately Marianne wouldn't listen to anyone, let alone her children. And that was if she remembered who they were.

'Let's go and see anyway.' Della put on a brave smile and corralled Marianne to come with her. She helped her downstairs, all the time chatting to her about this and that to try and take her mind off the watch.

Dementia.

At first Della had thought Marianne's confusion was because of the death of her father six months ago. She'd told Chris many times that it was due to the stress of losing Peter, the grief of being alone. But her parents had been keeping the rapid decline of Marianne's health between themselves, leaving Della and Chris to pick up the pieces after the funeral.

As Chris was married with a family, and Della was living alone, it seemed the easier choice for her to move out of her flat and back home to keep an eye on things. But she hadn't realised how exhausting it would be. She had to be switched on at all times, even during the night as Marianne had a tendency to wander off in her nightie. How she remembered the alarm code but not to put her slippers on was beyond her understanding.

They'd arranged for carers to come in twice a day while Della was at work. She'd recently been made redundant before getting the temporary contract at *Somerley News*, and she didn't want to lose that job, too. Going to work, being with other people every day was the only thing keeping her sane.

Chris, and Wendy, her sister-in-law, helped out as much as they could, but it would only be for a few hours every now and then. They'd take Marianne out to give Della time to be in the house alone, but she always felt guilty and ended up joining them.

Eventually, Della had gone to the doctors with Marianne, and their local GP, who they'd known for some time, ran a series of tests. It showed things had deteriorated rapidly, and nothing as they knew would be the same again.

The letter propped behind the carriage clock on the mantelpiece had been there for three weeks now. Della couldn't read it again.

Downstairs, she led Marianne back into the living room, where she'd been sitting when she'd left her, and searched around the armchair. Mum spent most of her days there now, either watching TV when she was lucid or staring out of the window with glazed eyes. It was horrendous never knowing from one day to the next which version Della would come home to.

Rummaging around the cushions, it didn't take long to find the watch. She held it in the air for Marianne to see.

'Found it.' Della smiled, not mentioning where it had been. Marianne might get upset because she wouldn't remember taking it off or be angry because Della didn't believe her when she'd said Chris had stolen it.

But Marianne had other ideas anyway.

'It was you!' she cried, snatching it from her. 'You took it earlier when I wasn't looking, and now you've put it back, so it doesn't seem as though you did. You nasty cow.'

Della swallowed her response and kept the smile on her face. 'You have it now, Mum. No harm done.'

'I think you should leave.'

Della wished that she could. 'I live here, Mum, remember?'

'Well, I want you out!'

Marianne launched herself at Della, grabbing handfuls of her hair and pulling hard.

Della cried out in pain, trying to prise her hands away. Still, Marianne held firm.

Tears burned Della's eyes. 'Stop it, Mum, please!'

All of a sudden, anger spent, Marianne released Della, gave her a filthy sneer, and sat down in the armchair again.

With a hand to her head, Della lowered herself onto the settee, waiting for the shaking in her body to settle. Her head was throbbing; no doubt she'd have lost some hair.

She couldn't go on like this, couldn't deal with angry outbreaks, the pouring out of such vitriol when she was trying to do her best. It was breaking her heart, feeling useless all the time. Yet what choice did she have?

She glanced at Marianne, her eyes firmly on the TV, watching the news, and acting as if nothing had happened.

Her mum sensed Della watching her and gave her the largest of grins. It took all of Della's strength to return it, but smile she did.

She waited for the carer to arrive, quickly telling her what had happened, although knowing for now Marianne would mostly sleep her little adventure off without recollection.

Then she set off to work. She would be twenty minutes late again.

## P IS FOR PATRICK

*The best day in my life is going to take a long time to get to. First I need to give you some details. I met Pat when I was eighteen. He worked in the Hope and Anchor, in Hope Street, and I came rushing in with a gaggle of girlfriends to catch last orders.*

*The Hope and Anchor was our usual Friday evening haunt, and if it wasn't for Vanda suggesting going into Hedworth first, we would have been in there all evening. But sometimes a change is as good as a rest, or so they say. We usually enjoy ourselves in town, but that night we were happy to get back. And it was karaoke night.*

*Pat was working the bar. I'd seen him there for a few Fridays, chatted to him when I got drinks in, whenever I could hear him over the noise. I didn't know much about him. Until then, I thought he wasn't interested in me. But then he asked me out.*

*Cue fifteen years later, we were married with three children. Things hadn't been going great, and our relationship was over. Neither of us wanted to finish things, but equally we couldn't live with each other anymore. Our youngest was ten and took it bad, but he was fine once things had settled down. We stayed in the family home, and Pat moved out.*

*Yet that in itself turned out to be our saving grace. Living apart for three years, we kept our family together. Those three children of ours, Ben, who I've already mentioned, Chrissie, twelve, and Emmy, fourteen, kept us talking. When you have children, you have to keep meeting up.*

*Gradually, after the bitterness subsided, Pat started coming in for coffee, then joining us for the odd family meal. One night when the kids were in their rooms, over a glass of wine, we realised we still had feelings for each other. We talked through how we'd let life get in the way of our happiness and that we wanted to try again.*

*That was two years ago, and last month, we were remarried. Our children were best man and bridesmaids, and we had a huge party to celebrate.*

*We were lucky to find our way back to each other. Times had been hard before, and when we were apart we realised what we'd had was special but not appreciated. Yet the love we shared was still there.*

*I'm delighted we're back together. I feel complete again. As for the kids, they're happy, too!*

*Thank you for giving me the opportunity to share my feelings.*
*Melissa Wright*

# CHAPTER FIFTEEN

Eve was sitting at the bottom of the garden on a bench, sharing the remains of a bottle of wine with Mack. The meal had gone well, and they were enjoying the last rays of sun. They'd been blessed with another warm day, after a sudden shower earlier in the morning.

The garden was looking lovely, despite it being Clark's domain. Not long after he'd died, Eve had attacked it with gusto one afternoon, when she couldn't bear to see it so messy, and found she really enjoyed it. The fruits of her labour could be seen in the colours surrounding them.

'Was your husband's death sudden?' Mack asked, taking a sip of wine afterwards.

They hadn't spoken much more in detail about their partners since they'd shared lunch, so his question took her by surprise. Eve wondered if Mack wanted to open up about his past.

She nodded. 'There was no warning at all, to my knowledge. He hadn't been feeling ill. There were no episodes of fatigue or breathlessness. One minute we were watching TV, and the next...' Eve paused. 'Actually, that isn't quite true. I went into the kitchen to get some snacks. I started looking at something on my phone, you know how it is, and was gone a few minutes longer than I was planning. When I went back into the living room, he was on the floor, clutching his chest. Seconds later, he dropped into unconsciousness and never woke up.'

'That must have been awful. I bet you blamed yourself for it, too?'

'I knew soon after there would have been nothing I could have done to save him but, at the time, yes, I did.' She shook her head. 'It was all I could think about. If only this, if only that. I became quite bitter for a while, and then, well, I just got on with life without Clark. There was nothing else I could do. Grace blamed herself, for a long time, too. She'd ummed and ahhed about whether to go out or not that evening, so when I rang her to tell her to come home, when she got here, she was angry.'

'Things like that are no one's fault.'

'I know. It's easy to see that now.'

'Do you still miss him?'

'Every day. They're such a huge part of your past, aren't they?'

Mack reached for her hand and gave it a squeeze. 'I don't know which is worse, to be fair,' he admitted. 'Losing someone without saying goodbye or watching them disappear through a long and debilitating illness to their death.'

'Is that what happened to your wife?'

'Kind of. She ended up taking her own life.'

Eve did her best to hide her shock. 'Oh, I'm sorry to hear that.'

'Yeah, it wasn't nice to go through, but me and the girls came out the other side.'

'How did it happen, do you mind me asking?' She touched his forearm, hoping to comfort him. 'You don't have to tell me if it's too painful to discuss.'

'No, it's fine.' He placed his own hand over hers and left it there. 'It was a few years ago now. Helen was bipolar and drank to rid herself of the dark days. We tried years to get her off the stuff, and it worked every now and then. But she'd always end up going back to it.

'I don't blame her entirely. I've never been addicted to anything, so I don't know what it's like to stop. But it was hell to go through, never knowing from one day to the next how she'd be when I got home from work.'

Eve could understand that. It had been the same for her, wondering if her dad would be in a good mood or not. Perhaps she should tell Mack that one day, but it wasn't the right time now.

'She got so tired of letting everyone down that she attempted suicide on several occasions,' he went on. 'We knew it was only a matter of time before she was successful. I felt so helpless, like I should have done more for her. But it was an illness, and she couldn't cope with it. Luckily for the girls, it was me who found her hanging in the garage.'

Even after all this time, Eve thought she knew Mack. Yet she hadn't realised what a sensitive person he was, or maybe that was how life had changed him. She would have done the same for Clark and would have hated it, too. At least her grief was because of him leaving her too suddenly.

'Oh, Mack, that must have been terrible to go through.'

He nodded, eyes glistening. 'In some ways it was easier when she'd gone. There was no one to drag us down with her then. I know that sounds harsh, but I wanted a better life than the one we shared. I promised myself when she died that I would live life to the full.'

'And have you?'

'For a while, that played with my emotions too much.' He shook his head. 'Since then, I haven't found anyone to do anything special with. I think I'm scared of caring for someone like that and then losing them again. It messed with my head for a long time.'

'Is that why you came back to Somerley?'

'Part of the reason.' He shrugged. 'I needed a fresh start. The kids are grown up with kids of their own, and I wanted to get some roots down. Catch up with old friends rather than making news ones. I think I made the right choice so far.'

She caught the look in his eye and smiled. 'So do I.'

'I really enjoy spending time with you, Eve,' he said, touching her cheek with his palm. 'It's been a brilliant evening. And, after all I've said, I feel as though I'm closer to you somehow. I hope you don't mind.'

'Not at all. It was great to talk and see something from a different perspective.'

'I know things have been hard for us, and we're both scared of getting hurt, but we, much more than others, know how quickly life can be taken away.' Mack swallowed. 'I told you about Helen because I'm developing feelings for you.'

'Oh.' She gazed into his eyes, thankful it wasn't dark enough not to see the compassion in them. Because she was feeling giddy all of a sudden. Was she falling for him, too?

She smiled shyly. 'How about we try not hanging on to the past, and move forwards with the future?'

'Yes, I'd like that. Shall I cook next time?'

'That sounds like a plan.'

'How about this Friday?'

'You're not coming to the party?'

'Which party?'

'Don't worry. You'll be told about it shortly, I'm sure.'

'Well, I don't think I can wait that long to do this.'

As he drew his head towards her, their lips touching at last, Eve didn't even think how alien it was to be kissing another man. She just thought of Mack and his touch, his gentleness. His hope for a better future.

# 1983

*My dearest Rose,*

*I hope this finds you well. It's the eve of my fortieth birthday, and I'm trying not to get too stressed about the surprise party planned for tomorrow evening. I know it should have been a secret, but I overheard Betty on the phone talking about getting everyone to the local pub before we arrived.*

*I wish I hadn't known about it to be fair, as I hate surprises, but at least I can practice my "shocked" expression before I go into the building.*

---

*I've left the above in the letter as I stopped writing it then and came back to it after the party. I wish I hadn't been so nervous about it as it was a really great evening. All my friends and family were there, lots of my work colleagues, and some who had left the factory, too.*

*I've been very fortunate to meet Betty, Rose. She is everything I love in a woman. Everything I had hoped I'd have with you. It sounds terrible for me to say that I love her so very much, because it almost makes her seem like she is second best. She isn't. I just wanted you to know that I think about what could have been between you and I with fond memories.*

*Michael is sixteen now and about to start a Youth Training Scheme. Rachel is fourteen and doing well at school. And then there's Charlotte who is our baby at nine years old. That is definitely it for our family. We are happy with the three. Betty is retraining as a midwife, now the children can almost fend for themselves.*

*I'm still working at the factory. I'm the head of overall production, meaning I have three teams and over one hundred staff to manage. I tell you, once you get to this level, most of the work I do is about crisis management with the workers! The machines and production side of things are the least of it. But we do try to keep a happy work environment. It seems to be working as the firm have just won Employer of the Year. I am so proud of everyone.*

*It's a habit now for me to write to you each birthday. I'm not sure why but I feel it keeps me close to you, without being unfaithful. I hope you are happy.*

*Again, I wonder how many children you have now, Rose. How they have been moulded by your spirit and love. I only hope that you're as happy with Harry as I am with Betty. Family means everything to me.*

*All my love,*
*Cedric*

## **CHAPTER SIXTEEN**

It was two weeks since Grace's first article had gone out and the letters had trickled in. So far, there were seven, and she was having trouble filling the two-page spread Tom had kept back for her. At this rate, she'd have to write some letters herself to include.

'What am I going to do?' she asked her mum that morning over breakfast. 'I can't write about nothing. I was hoping to have at least twenty letters to choose from.'

'It's a start, Grace,' Eve encouraged. 'Don't be disheartened. You have to get people to want to send in their letters.'

'How?'

'You can write more articles.'

'I'm already doing that. I have a great story lined up about a little girl and her dog. Plus there is a couple willing to be interviewed about their baby. He was born with a hole in his heart, and their best day was when he had surgery to repair it. He's two now.'

'You see, that's the kind of heart-warming story you're good at writing.' Eve reached across the table to give Grace's hand a squeeze. 'You'll be fine. Have you asked your gran to write a letter?'

'Yes, but she's refusing so far. What about you?'

'What about me?' Eve pulled back her hand.

'You must have a best day in your life.' Grace stared at her. 'It had better be when I was born.'

'Oh, of course.' Eve screwed up her face.

Grace giggled. 'I bet we'll have lots of letters about the same life occasions.'

'I'm sure you will. Most things happen to people rather than us creating memories by following our dreams.'

'I'd settle for those at the moment.'

'Don't worry, love. It will take off, I'm sure.'

Grace wished she had her mum's optimism. She didn't want to give the project time to fail, not as it was her idea. She'd have to drum up some press herself.

'I think I'll start calling some of my contacts,' she said. 'Do a bit of brainstorming. See if I can get a few more prizes to give away.'

'That's my girl. Your dad would have been so proud of you.' Eve put her hands on the table. 'Right, I'd better be off.' She pushed herself to standing. 'Want me to ask Gran again, see if she'll join in?'

'Please.'

'You'll be fine, whatever happens.' Eve kissed Grace on her forehead before leaving. 'I have faith in you.'

At work, Grace found a small pile of post on her desk. She dived on it, to find a mere three letters that were for the project. She tossed them to one side, not even wanting to look at them right now. However, after their daily briefing, she read them and found they were quite amusing.

They were all different. One was three pages long, the others barely a couple of hundred words. But they were stories about the folk of Somerley. And from what she had read today, they were all light-hearted, warming, and would bring pleasure to anyone who read them. Still, she went to moan to Flora who was in reception.

'Three paltry letters,' she cried, perching her bottom on the side of Flora's desk. 'I went out of my way to make an idiot of myself on live radio and—'

'You didn't make an idiot of yourself.'

'That's not the point, I might have.'

'What will you do if you don't get many?'

'If people won't join in, I can't force them. But so far, I've had fifteen wedding days, two christenings, *so* many big birthdays and a funeral.'

'A funeral?' Flora screwed up her face.

'It was for a cat! They buried it in the garden, giving it a guard of honour with daffodils and made a headstone. I thought it was a bit morbid myself, but I have to be objective. It's not my best day. It's theirs.'

While she was there, Grace read one out loud. 'The best day of my life was when I won five thousand pounds on a scratch card. Me and my missus had been arguing, and she hadn't given me money for her share. We always got four scratch cards a week, paid for two apiece. Well, I bought four, and one came up.'

'Ha!' Flora giggled.

'You should have seen her face when I told her I'd won,' Grace went on, 'and that the winnings were mine as she hadn't paid towards them. I refrained from laughing for as long as I could. She took it in good faith, but she walloped me around the arm when I said I was joking. We saved half and used the other for a holiday. It was just what we needed.'

'Aw.'

'We still do the lottery each week and get those scratch cards on the off chance we'll win again. She pays me promptly every week now, though. That's from Mr Dave Scarrett.'

'That's a funny one. What would your best day be, Grace?'

'I have lots of things I could put forward, but I'm not saying anything about them. I'm saving them for the very last week of the project.'

'Spoilsport.'

They both looked up as the front doors opened automatically.

'Special delivery!' Tyler cried, walking across to them. He was carrying a post sack, which he placed on the reception counter with a bang. He smiled at Flora before saying hello to Grace.

'Here you go, ye of little faith.' He pointed to the bag. 'Have a look in there.'

'What is it?' She pulled it towards her, peeped inside, and then squealed. 'Letters!' She took out a handful. 'Lots and lots of letters.' She grinned at Tyler. 'Did these come in overnight?'

'They did.'

'Wow.'

'Wow indeed.' Flora was placing the envelopes in a pile. 'There must be at least fifty.'

'Sixty-one to be precise,' Tyler told her.

Grace was agog. 'You counted them?'

'I sorted them especially for you this morning. That's why they didn't come with the normal mail run.'

'You are amazing.' Grace couldn't help herself. She ran around to the public side of the counter and threw her arms around his neck. 'Thank you!'

Tyler blushed a little. 'Anything for you, my love.'

Behind them, Flora sniggered.

Grace picked the envelopes up that Flora had bundled together. They were mostly white, but there were the odd red and pink ones. 'I can't wait to get started on these.'

'Perhaps you can tell me all about them over lunch?' Tyler suggested.

'That would be my pleasure.'

'Great, I'll be back at one?'

'Perfect. And thanks again for bringing these to me.'

Grace watched Tyler until he'd left the building and then noticed Flora staring at her, arms folded.

'What?' she asked.

'He really cares about you.'

'I know. We've been friends for ages now.'

'No, I mean he *really* cares about you.'

'Me and Tyler?' Grace frowned. 'I don't think so.'

Flora raised her eyebrows.

'We're just good friends,' Grace insisted.

Flora leaned forwards. 'I like him, though. Great eye candy and a real gent with it.'

'Then you date him.'

'Oh, no. He only has eyes for you.'

'We've known each other since forever, and nothing's happened before now.'

Flora paused. 'There's your letter then, right there. The best day of your life will be when you kiss Tyler.'

Grace was about to protest, but the phone rang, and Flora reached to answer it. She shook her head before going back into the main room. She and Tyler were friends, no more, no less. Weren't they?

## S IS FOR SCHOOL

*I wasn't very bright at school. In fact, you could say I was the class clown. The one who always wanted to make people laugh.*

*Do you often wonder why you wasted so much school time? I know I did, once I'd been gone a few years. I had a path which I wanted to travel along but I never knuckled down enough to get the grades I needed. I was too busy messing around with my friends.*

*But on the last day at school, my form teacher, Mr Collins, pulled me to one side and gave me a talking-to. We had a long chat, and I told him about how it was at home.*

*I didn't have the best start in life. I'd been told I was useless and wouldn't amount to anything for most of my early years. In the end, I lived up to that. Nature versus nurture, hmm.*

*Mr Collins said he had seen something special in me. I think he was the first adult to see my potential. He complimented me on my graphic design skills, my computer skills, and even my English essays. He said I should think about going to college, that it wasn't too late to change things around.*

*For once in my life, thank goodness I listened. I left my mates behind at the school gates and headed for Hedworth Polytechnic. I took a few courses and then I went to university.*

*Now, I'm a web designer and marketer for a large company, and I love my job.*

*That's another thing Mr Collins said to me. Don't do what you're good at just to chase the money. Do what you're passionate about and the money will follow.*

*Thank you, Mr Collins, for turning my life around.*
*Simon Tilsdale*

# CHAPTER SEVENTEEN

Friday evening had come round slowly for Eve, but now it was finally here. She and Mack had bumped into each other a few times at work, had the odd coffee, and the chatter through their messages on their phones had been going backwards and forwards. It had been so much fun and made her think how much they'd missed out on when they were younger. It must have been wonderful to give someone a mobile phone number and flirt with them online.

She gave a twirl as she admired herself in the mirror on the wardrobe. Not bad, she mused. She'd chosen a woollen dress with three-quarter-length sleeves. It was still warm for late August, but was getting chillier at night-time.

'You look pretty. Where are you off to, all dolled up?' Grace asked her when she came downstairs.

'There's a party at Somerley Heights. Francis is eighty.' Eve grinned. 'Want to come?'

'No thanks.' Grace shuddered. 'There is nothing I'd like less.'

'You young ones don't know you're born. I bet they'll drink far more than if they were younger. I've never seen a bunch of old ones put it back so much. They love their whisky and sherry. Hence.' She went into the kitchen and came back with two bags, bottles clanking inside one of them.

'Well, enjoy!' Grace shooed her from the room. 'Don't keep the man waiting.'

Eve was halfway out of the door when she turned back and smiled. 'Thanks, kiddo. Have to make an effort, even getting down with the *olds*.'

'If you're trying to mimic my generation, I'd give up now.'

'See you later. Don't wait up!'

There was drizzle in the air, so Eve raced to the car, trying to dodge it before it got to her hair. She only needed a few drops, and it would frizz catastrophically. She glanced in the rear-view mirror, taking one last look for rogue mascara and lipstick on her teeth.

The party was in full swing when she arrived. It was set out in the large communal hall. All the chairs had been pushed to the walls, creating a large space in the middle. A man from the next village was playing the piano. Eve knew there would be a singalong later in the evening, but for now, the music tinkled as a soothing backdrop.

There were so many people there it was hard to spot Rose, so she popped the food onto the table laid out for the buffet. As was usual, everyone had a list to look at beforehand, an item to tick off so that nothing was missed off or duplicated, and they weren't left with too many sandwiches and not enough cakes.

Eve had opted for sausage rolls and pork pies this time. Easy to prepare and plate up. She'd also bought along several dips and a bowl of coleslaw.

'There you are.' Rose appeared by her side. 'I thought you were never coming.'

'I did say about seven.'

Rose waved away her comment. 'I've been here since five.'

'Yes, I can tell.' Eve noticed she was already unsteady on her feet.

'Come and sit with me once you've got a drink,' Rose spoke over her shoulder as she walked away.

Eve headed over to the far corner. Sitting with her mum wasn't the first place she'd anticipated going. So seeing Mack stacking cans of lager on the table made her smile.

He was dressed in a short-sleeved pale-blue shirt and dark denim jeans, the sandy-coloured boots on his feet similar to the ones he wore at work. He smiled when he spotted her, eyes twinkling with warmth.

'Yes, madam.' He grinned. 'What can I get you?'

Eve couldn't help but laugh. 'They roped you into being the barman?'

Mack frowned. 'They said everyone new has to take a turn...' He smiled then. 'Have I been had?'

'I'm afraid so. But I will have a glass of something cold.'

'Wine?'

'Lemonade, please.' She handed over the bottles she'd brought along. 'Driving.'

'Any chance of a top-up?' Rose shouted over to Mack, holding up her empty glass.

Eve smirked. 'You see? You've started something now.'

'Maybe. But I think you'll have to man the *bar* while I do the refills. I don't trust this lot not to help themselves to it all.'

Eve watched with interest his interaction with everyone. In a matter of seconds, they were all roaring with laughter at something he'd said. It made her smile even more.

She ended up staying with him for the next hour, happily chatting between rounds of songs on the piano, which were getting louder and quicker with each tune. Open mike was a thing here, as was singing songs from days gone by.

She was leaning on the windowsill next to Mack as the pianist was cheered before he left for the evening.

'I suppose that's it,' Mack said. 'But you were right, they do know how to have fun. I haven't laughed so much in a long time.'

'Oh, it's not over yet.' Eve shook her head. 'In fact, it's just beginning.'

Rose was putting on a playlist. A song from the sixties burst out, and people began to get up and dance.

'Quite spritely for their ages, aren't they?' Mack pointed to the birthday boy, eighty-year-old Francis, who was doing some kind of jive with Rose.

'They are. I hope I'm like my mum when I grow older.'

'Beautiful, intelligent, and kind?'

Eve nudged him, blushing at his compliment. His eyes returned to the dancers, and she stared at him surreptitiously. She still remembered that teenager she'd fallen in love with. The one who'd broken her heart when he'd left.

The music changed to a slower tempo, and Mack held out his hand. 'Care to dance?'

They joined the crowd on the makeshift dance floor. It was hot and sticky after the recent storm, the doors to the garden flung open to make up for it. She wanted to rest her head on his shoulder, but what they were doing now would set the tongues wagging regardless.

There was no need for words as even with the music playing, a comfortable silence dropped between them. It was as if the years were rolling back.

She'd had a good life with Clark, but she couldn't help wondering what if she'd gone to university with Mack. There was no guarantee they'd been able to get in the same one, but what if they had? What if they'd gone on to live together, get married, have children of their own?

But then again, she wouldn't be feeling how she was right

now. That maybe she was being given a second chance with Mack. And if so, she was going to take it.

His lips were inches away from hers, and if she wasn't in the middle of a group of rowdy pensioners she might have kissed him. Instead, she smiled when the music changed, and they went back to their corner. Just in time for everyone to rush up for last orders.

## CHAPTER EIGHTEEN

It was nearly four weeks since the project had started and, much to Grace's relief, the letters were beginning to fly in. Most were delivered by post, but as Somerley was a small town, a lot had been dropped off by hand, too.

Each morning, Grace would go through them all, logging down the details, discussing with the team what they would or wouldn't print. There were lots of stories to follow up on, and she was enjoying herself immensely.

She was chatting to Joe about TV the night before.

'I quite fancy myself as a cop,' Joe had said after telling her he'd caught up on the latest episode of *Vera*. 'If you think about it, it isn't much different to what we do. We go out and interview people, scope out the best bits, spit out the lies and the libel cases and even bring people to justice when we do exposés.'

'Yes, if only we could arrest people as well, we'd have the power to be invincible.' Grace shook her head, smiling. 'It's nothing like being a detective, Joe.'

'I'm going to do that when I retire.'

'Become a cop?' she teased.

'Partly. I'm going to write a crime thriller.'

Grace's head shot up for a moment. 'How come you've never mentioned that before?'

'Because I didn't want to tell anyone.'

'Why not?'

'Pipe dream, and all that. But then I'll have more time, and I'll have to do something with my days, so I'm going to give it a go.'

'I think that's a great idea. Do you have any thoughts on plots or characters?'

'Maybe an older detective with a penchant for greasy food that he always spills down his tie, with a wayward dog and a stroppy ex-wife.'

'Fiona might not be too happy about that!' Grace took the last letter from its envelope. She unfolded it and read the words. The blood drained from her face.

'I won't... what's wrong?'

She passed the letter to him.

*You're lucky that no one knows the real truth about you.*' Joe frowned. 'What does that mean?'

'I don't know.' Grace glanced over the envelope for clues, but there was no stamp on it. 'It was hand-delivered.'

'In that case, it would have been picked up on our CCTV.' Joe stood up to go over to the monitor.

'We don't know what time, though,' Grace said. 'It'll take ages to view it all.'

'We'll take it in turns until we find out. Who would do such a thing?'

'I've been feeling positive about this project, too.' Grace blinked away tears. 'I suppose there's always a pile of nutty letters. I had hoped that everyone would be happy to contribute something nice, not downright nasty. But this is the *Somerley News*, and I've been here before.'

'*This* is different, Grace. It isn't some random shouting

obscenities down the phone to get your attention. It's tantamount to a threat.'

'No, it isn't.' She batted away his comment. 'It's someone trying to get attention. Perhaps they think we'll print it, which we won't. Just ignore it.'

'If you're sure.' Joe sat down again.

'I'm sure.' Grace screwed up the letter and put it in the bin.

'I'd save that, if I were you. It might be needed as evidence later.'

'You've been watching too much *Vera*.'

'Even so, humour an old man and keep it.'

She sighed, and with great aplomb, got it out of the bin and popped it in her desk drawer. 'Okay now?'

Joe nodded.

Grace got back to her work, but she couldn't help thinking about the letter. She went through to reception to speak to Flora. Like Joe said, it was probably something and nothing, but it had upset her a little, nonetheless.

'Hey, my friend.' Flora grinned, then pouted. 'No mug of tea? Your standards are dropping.'

Grace couldn't even muster a smile. She told Flora what had happened.

Flora shook her head in disbelief. 'Are you okay?'

Hearing her concern made Grace feel teary about the whole thing, and she hadn't been expecting that.

'I will be,' she said. 'It just threw me a little after all the nice letters coming in.'

'Some people are knobs. You shouldn't let it get to you.'

'I hadn't – well, until I spoke to you anyway.'

'What's been said in the office?'

'Only you and Joe know. I don't want anyone else to find out yet.'

'My lips are sealed, if you think that's wise.'

'It might be a one-off. I binned the letter, though, but Joe made me get it out and keep it.'

'Too right.'

Grace needed some fresh air. 'I'm going to grab some lunch for later. Do you want anything bringing back?'

'No, thanks. Are you sure you're okay?'

'Nothing that a cream cake can't make better.'

*Somerley News* was located on the left side of Somerley Square. When the newspaper was published every weekday, their head office had been in Hedworth, but now there was half the staff in numbers, they were in the heart of the town.

Grace bought a takeaway sandwich from The Coffee Stop and then went to sit under the oak tree in the centre of the square. She glanced around, spotting people she knew going about their daily business. Were any of them responsible for sending the letter?

She was being ridiculous, of course they weren't. But how would she know who could be so nasty?

And what was meant by the message? *You're lucky that no one knows the real truth about you.* What did that even mean?

Grace had no dark secrets in her closet. The only terrible thing she'd done in her life was shoplift sweets from Somerley Stores, and she reckoned most kids in the area would have done the same.

But the more she thought about it, the more she had her suspicions who was behind this.

It had to be Liam.

She got out her phone and rang him. 'Just what is your problem?' she said when he answered.

'Hello to you, too.'

'You couldn't bear to see me happy, could you? You had to try and spoil things for me.'

'I don't know what you mean.'

'The letter I got this morning. It was you, wasn't it? You

must have seen my project in the paper and sent it for a laugh. Well, it isn't funny.'

'Wait, what are you accusing me of?' Liam laughed. 'Don't you think I've got better things to do than play tricks on you?'

'It was cruel enough to be you.'

'What did it say?'

She paused, blindsided by his need to know when she thought he'd sent it. 'Never you mind,' she replied.

'Look, whatever's going on, I haven't sent you anything. So you have a nerve calling me and saying that—'

Grace disconnected the call, out of embarrassment in case she was wrong rather than anger. It had to be him, because if wasn't, then who could it be?

No, like she'd told Joe, she needed to put this out of her mind and get on with her job. She wouldn't let that lowlife creep put her off what she did best. Project One Letter was what she needed to devote her time to.

# L IS FOR LILY MORTIMER

*I remember the first day I came to Somerley. I had a job interview to work at a coffee shop that was in the middle of a renovation. It seemed pretty apt as my marriage had broken down. I needed time away, somewhere else to live for a while.*

*When I arrived in Somerley Square and saw the state of the premises, my heart sank. There was a lot of work to do. I'm not partial to getting my hands dirty but I was leaving a well-paid job. Was I right or was I a fool? But then I met Lily Mortimer, and she put my mind at rest.*

*I took a chance on a job I didn't know if I'd enjoy, or could even do, so that I could have a fresh start.*

*During the course of a couple of months, the wreck of a shell from the old Lil's Pantry was transformed into The Coffee Stop. I met Chloe, and we began to work and live together immediately. It was taxing at times, growing a business as well as learning to be single again. My life seemed to be falling apart... and then it wasn't.*

*Now many years later, I'm remarried, with a little boy, Rueben, and there is nowhere else I would rather live than here with them. Chloe and I are now joint owners of The Coffee Stop. It's been expanded to incorporate a book shop, and we have plans for an extra room and a licensed bar upstairs for private functions.*

*All this wouldn't have been possible without Lily Mortimer having faith in me that very first day we met. I'm forever grateful to her for changing the path of my life completely and making me into a businesswoman who I never knew I could be.*

*I'm glad I made my home here.*
*Kate Taylor*

## CHAPTER NINETEEN

Since the party at Somerley Heights, Eve hadn't been able to stop thinking about Mack. It was getting to the point that she almost felt like she had a schoolgirl crush on him again.

She thought of his words, going over each sentence. Remembered the feel of his arms around her when they'd danced. The urge to kiss him was still strong and, if it wasn't for her feeling shy, him too by the look of things, she might have enjoyed spending the night with him.

Something else was starting to invade her thoughts, too. The S.E.X. Oh, she knew it would probably be like riding a bike, but it wasn't that which scared her. It was the thought of her fifty-four-year-old body not being up to scratch. It would certainly be nothing like the one she had shared with Mack in her teens.

Then again, she expected he'd have the same kind of hang-ups. It was going to be strange, but the anticipation was there. The slow build-up had been nice.

Remembering something, Eve jumped up from the settee and dashed upstairs. She retrieved a stool from Grace's bedroom and the loft pole from her own. Then she opened the hatch and stretched for the ladder. Carefully, she stepped up and into the loft, flicking on the switch to her right.

Except for the Christmas tree and decorations, Eve hadn't been up there for a while. It had taken her six months until she'd felt able to sort through Clark's belongings to decide which to keep and which to give to the charity shop on the high street. Eventually, she'd filled two suitcases and three tea chests with his personal effects and pushed them to the space furthest away, out of sight.

But it wasn't these she was after that evening.

It took her a few minutes to locate the shoe box, but finally she spotted it. She pulled it down and sat on the floor, thankful that Clark had boarded the room out as soon as they'd moved in, to give them extra storage space.

Written in black marker pen was "Somerley High School 1985". She lifted the lid, wondering what treasures she'd find inside that she could share with Mack. There were bound to be some horrors among them.

The first thing she saw was an old diary. Her hands fell on it greedily, and she smiled as she flicked through its pages. It was full of teenage angst and notes about several boys she'd taken a shine to before getting together with Mack.

Over the years, she'd seen all but one of them mentioned still living in Somerley. She wondered what had happened to the one who'd got away. Had he been ambitious enough to leave and do something good? She made a mental note to Google him to see what he was up to.

Her hand clasped around a wooden ruler, recalling her old maths teacher slapping a similar one across fingers and backs of hands if anyone wasn't paying attention in his class. She'd written her name, and lots of her friends' names, all over it. You could barely see any other markings for blue ink.

On the last day of school, everyone had scrawled their names on each other's school shirts, too. The day itself had been mixed with happiness and excitement, and yet tinged with sadness, so it was a nice memento of a time in her life where she was leaving what she was used to and going out into the wild world.

But her dad had been livid when she'd got home. He'd called her a vandal, insisting she put it in the wash to sort it out. No matter how much she protested, he'd ignored her. The ink ensured it came out a dirty denim colour with darker smudges over it. She realised now he'd just wanted to ruin the memory.

Finally, she found the envelope she was after. Her legs beginning to ache, she decided to take it downstairs and grab a glass of red to sift through its contents in comfort.

Wine poured, legs outstretched on the settee, she took out the first batch of photos. There were so many of her and her friends, then with some of the boys they knew from school.

She found a few of her and Mack. She could clearly see they liked each other. There was one of them in a group sitting on and around a bench in the school playground, all trying to make their uniform a little different. Rolled up skirts and shortened ties. Hair in mullets for the boys and permed curls for the girls.

She snorted at the sight of herself on one of them. Mack had cuddled up close and thrown his arm around her shoulder. Her goofy grin had been caught on camera for all to see. Even then, she'd been smitten with him.

Another one where they were hanging around the oak tree in Somerley Square. Another when they were sunbathing in the park, always as part of a larger group.

She laughed when she spotted one with them in fancy dress at an eighteenth birthday party. They'd gone as Morticia and Gomez Addams. Eve looked fetching in a long black wig and flowing dress, her face painted white with black lipstick, thick false eyelashes, and lots of eyeliner. Mack had slicked his hair to one side, painted on a moustache, and borrowed his brothers suit and a cravat.

She was making a pile of what to take with her when she spotted a smaller white envelope. Inside it was a handwritten letter.

*Dear Eve,*

*I can't believe this is the last time I'll see you until half-term in October. I wish you were coming with me. You have so much to offer, and there are plenty of courses you could have got on. I will miss you so much.*

*I am excited, though, and will tell you all about it when I get back. The digs are amazing, and I can't wait to settle in. And find the best pubs, ha!*

*Peace, Mack.*

Memories of that last night came rushing to her. They'd gone out with a group of friends, and when he'd dropped her off, she'd clung to him, not wanting to let him go. He said he'd be back and then he'd given her the note to read on her own.

Eve sighed. It was clear to her now that, even in that last letter, he was thinking of moving on without her. The world had been waiting for him, and he it. If only she hadn't been so browbeaten by her father.

Mack hadn't come home at half-term as planned. He'd just about managed a couple of days at Christmas before shooting back to uni again. Their relationship had petered out after that.

Eve remembered him ringing her to say they should cool things. Not that they were even warm. She hadn't seen him in so long and knew it was over. But she hadn't wanted to admit it. She wanted to still be loved by him.

Instead, she'd ploughed everything into her business studies course at college, and despite her father's protests, had started weekly art and craft evening classes. It was there she'd found her love for sewing.

Was it a good time to ignite the relationship, she mused? Was she prepared to lose Mack all over again?

Or, as he might only be here on a temporary basis, would she be better letting the past stay in the past?

# 1993

*My dearest Rose,*

*I hope this finds you well. Where are the years going? I mean, the big five-o. How did that happen?*

*Betty and I have moved again. As our brood have all flown the nest, we decided to relocate to somewhere a little more off the beaten track. We live off a lane now, half a mile from the nearest house, and I've never been happier.*

*I thought I might hate it away from the town, but it's great. We have a little smallholding. Nothing special, but we have chickens, miniature goats, and a rescue donkey called Clyde who thinks he rules the place. He's so loud!*

*Michael is married now, just last month. He and his wife, Katie, both work for the NHS. Michael is coming up to his final year as a junior doctor, and Katie is an A&E staff nurse. They do a lot of shift work between them, but they seem happy.*

*Rachel is engaged to be married, but she and Denton want to wait a few years before they tie the knot. They're in Australia at the moment. After she got her degree in Sociology, she headed down under. That's where she met Denton, he's an Aussie.*

*Betty and I really miss having her around, but I'm quite pleased that one of our children has got the travelling bug. My dislike for flying means that we don't do any long-haul flights. One day, perhaps.*

*And our Charlotte, the baby in the family. She's at Newcastle University at the moment, reading English and Media Studies. She has a real artistic flair.*

*How we had such different children is beyond me, but it's nice to see them branching out on their own. Having said that, I can't wait until one of them makes me a granddad.*

*I'd like to think that you'd love it here, Rose. It's a fifteen-minute walk to the village, where there is a pub, a small row of shops, a church, a school, and an Italian restaurant. It's so tiny and quaint, and yet we love it for that. We've settled in with the locals and made more friends. It's been a good move for us both.*

*All my love,*
*Cedric*

## CHAPTER TWENTY

Della pulled the car into the drive, switched off the engine, and sat there for a moment. She glanced at the house, her childhood home, recalling happier times when she'd rushed through its front door. Shouting about excited days out, exam results she'd been proud of. Coming home from a date and her mum waiting to ask her about it. Her first week at school, college, university, and then work. Christmas dinners, birthday lunches, family gatherings.

Now she wondered what delights would be waiting for her inside.

Would her mum be talkative, responsive, and fun to be with?

Or would she be angry with her again, ready to rip out her eyes, hit her with anything to hand?

It had been terrible but a necessary evil going through the house to rid it of unseen dangers. Things that had been there for years as useful items now became potential weapons she had to be wary of. Knives Marianne could cut herself, or Della, with. Hardback books she could sling at her. In the kitchen, locks on cupboard doors, most of the time the kettle hidden away. Saucepans out of reach unless there was someone who needed to use them. Having said that, her mum might be getting frail, but she could pack a mean punch if she felt threatened.

Finally, she dragged herself out of her car, let herself into the house, and shouted through to Marianne.

'Hi, Mum, only me. Would you like a cuppa, or have you had one recently?' Della knew Marianne might not answer but had been told to react how she would if everything was normal.

Normal, what was that anymore?

She sighed into the silence, shrugging off her jacket and removing her shoes. She went into the living room, thinking she would find an empty chair, but Marianne was sitting in it. Her eyes seemed glazed as if she was miles away but yet staring at the TV.

'Mum?' she said softly, moving to stand in front of her. She'd learned the hard way not to touch her arm after being hit in the face a couple of times.

'Oh, hello, love.' Marianne's smile was faint.

'What are you watching, anything good?'

'Just the usual.' She ushered Della out of the way, her eyes back to the TV in seconds.

Della picked up the beaker from the table beside her. 'A cup of tea?' she offered again.

'Your father has not long made me one. It was lovely, with lots of sugar, just how he knows I like it. Not how you make it, like gnat's piss.'

The hostility in her voice shocked Della at times, but she'd long ago realised she shouldn't take it personally, no matter how much it stung. As soon as the words had been uttered, Marianne probably wouldn't remember whether she'd said she loved Della or wanted to harm her. But Marianne had never sworn in her earlier years, well, never in front of Della and Chris anyway. So it jarred to hear it now.

She took the beaker into the kitchen regardless. The room was tidy, so she suspected Marianne hadn't moved from the chair since one of the carers had come in at lunch time. Her shoulders sagged: she'd better check the chair wasn't wet when she went back into the room.

There was a pile of post on the side, and she rifled through it. Spotting an official one, she opened it, her heart racing wildly before she'd even got halfway through reading it. Her legs went all weak, so she pulled out a chair to sit at the table. She read the letter again, slower this time, to take it all in.

Mum was getting worse. Towards the end, her consultant was even suggesting that residential care could be a safer option for her.

How dare they think Della wasn't capable of looking after her own mother.

It would break her to see this happen, but equally, Della couldn't cope much longer, unless she gave up her job.

Another envelope caught her eye, and she reached inside it to find a voucher, money off a holiday if it was booked within the next two weeks.

Della harrumphed. She hadn't been overseas in three years now. Hadn't even taken a short break. She desperately needed a holiday. Somewhere she could lounge beside a pool with a trashy novel and a large glass of something cool, doing her own version of Shirley Valentine. Running away from her problems, yet knowing they'd still be there on her return.

'Della, what the hell are you doing in the kitchen?' Marianne screeched. 'Where's my tea?'

Della sighed and stood up. She placed the letters in a pile to read later. 'Coming, Mum,' she shouted through. So much for her not wanting a hot drink.

A few minutes later, she took in the tea.

'There you are, Mum.' She held out the beaker for her. 'Are you hungry? I have your favourite doughnuts.'

'I've never liked doughnuts, silly girl.'

No matter what she'd been told, Della couldn't raise a smile this time.

## CHAPTER TWENTY-ONE

As Grace rushed along the path towards the entrance to *Somerley News* that morning, someone stepped out in front of her.

It was Liam. She jumped, holding a hand to her chest.

'You almost scared the life out of me. What are you doing creeping around like that?'

'You weren't looking where you were going.' He sneered. 'In a world of your own, as usual.'

Grace glared at him, then tried to get around him. But he blocked her way.

'What do you want?' she asked.

'I saw that letter you wrote about me. How could you print that in the paper?'

Grace's brow furrowed. 'I haven't written anything yet, never mind about you.'

'It was about the day we went to the seaside.'

'What?' Grace cast her mind back. The letter he was referring to was about a day trip from a man, about his partner before they'd decided to go their separate ways. It had been quite moving, how they'd realised their relationship was over and wanted to spend one last day together as something to hold on to as a good memory. There weren't many couples who would do that.

And she and Liam were one of the ones who wouldn't.

'That was nothing like how we parted, though, was it?' she said.

Grace recalled the night she'd got home from work and Liam had been sitting on the settee, face like thunder.

'Sorry I'm so late,' she'd said, removing her jacket and shoes, rubbing at her aching feet. 'The restaurant was busier than usual, and we had to wait ages for service. Did you enjoy the food I left for you?'

'Oh, yeah, sure. While you were gallivanting out, sharing fresh pasta and eating Tiramisu, I had to settle for a microwave meal for one and a yoghurt.'

'You didn't *have* to settle for that, you were invited along, too. And it wasn't a ready meal just because you had to heat it up. I made it from scratch yesterday, just the way you like it.'

'Only because you felt guilty.' He'd folded his arms, his eyes on the TV screen.

'I have nothing to *feel* guilty about.' She'd sighed. 'Can we not do this again, Liam? It's late, and I'm shattered.'

'You're always tired because you're never in early enough.'

'I've been out to a friend's fortieth birthday. I'm allowed to do that.'

'Not when I'm fed up sitting here all night on my own.'

'If you hadn't been pulling your face about it, you would have enjoyed it.'

'With your friends? I doubt it.'

'What is wrong with you? Why are you always so… angry?'

'Because you prefer going out to staying in with me.'

'That's not true, apart from when you're moaning. Besides, you hate coming out with me now, so the same applies to you.'

'That's because you prefer to go out with others and not me.'

'I asked if you wanted to come to the cinema with me last week!'

'So you could do a review for the paper. How romantic is that?'

'And then we had tickets for the theatre.'

'To watch *Dirty Dancing*?' He'd rolled his eyes.

'There were lots of men there with their partners.'

'Not my type of thing, and again, only for your job.'

'I like the perks. You used to, when we first met.'

'Yeah, well, that was then, and this is now.'

'What do you mean by that?'

'I'm sick of playing second fiddle to your job. You're out most evenings because of it, and I'm fed up of being on my own.'

'*You're* the reason you're so miserable as you don't want to do anything,' she'd snapped, unable to keep her temper at bay any longer.

'I end up sitting on my own. It's no fun.'

Grace had paused, trying to calm down. The last thing she wanted was for them to go to bed on another argument.

'It's part of my job to cover some events,' she'd said eventually. 'I'll try and get less for a couple of weeks so we can go out together, but you know there will be more things going on over the summer months.'

He'd shaken his head. 'I can't do this anymore.'

And that had been that. Grace hadn't been able to persuade him otherwise. She'd moved out the weekend after.

Funnily enough, she hadn't missed Liam for long and, seeing him now, angry and sulky like a petulant child, she was beginning to understand why.

'You've made it up to get back at me, haven't you?' he

went on as the people of Somerley went about their business around them.

One of the delivery vans headed for the car park at the back of the market, music blasting out of an open window.

'Now you're being paranoid.' Grace stepped to the side to get past, but he did the same, blocking her once more.

'Some of the things in that letter are memories we shared. Did you write it as a subliminal message for me, so that we could get back together?'

'I didn't write it. And actually, I wouldn't do that. I know there's no chance, so why would I even try?'

Liam huffed. 'I suppose you were okay until someone better came along.'

His words brought sudden tears to her eyes, and she blinked rapidly to stop them from falling. She wouldn't cry in front of him. Not anymore.

'Look, I don't know what your game is but—'

'She's named Rebecca, or Becks as I call her. You might know her, actually. She used to be in your year at school. She says she remembers you as the geeky kid with the skinny legs and flat chest. Not much changed there when you grew up, did it?'

'It *was* you who sent that nasty note!' Grace shook her head in disgust.

'Not that again. I wouldn't waste my ink on you nowadays.'

'Then why are you so certain I would waste my words on you? Now, shove off and leave me alone.' Grace pushed past Liam then, leaving his words behind but not until she'd heard a torrid stream of horrible things.

How could he be so nasty? He'd searched her out, for what? After so long, she wasn't really sure. What had she ever seen in him?

She stepped into the reception area to see Flora setting up for the day.

Flora eyed Grace's expression and came out from behind the desk. 'What's wrong?' she asked, all concerned. 'You look like you've seen a ghost.'

'I think I have. Can I sit with you for a couple of minutes before going through?'

'Of course.'

As Flora beckoned her forwards, Grace glanced over her shoulder. She expected to see Liam there, glaring at her to make a point. But he'd gone.

What on earth was his game? Did he want to make her feel sorry for something she didn't know she'd done? Or did he want her to know that he'd moved on, when he thought she clearly hadn't?

Well, that had changed now. Because she *had* moved on. She was over Liam, more annoyed that she'd let him walk over her for years. And she loathed him with a passion because of it.

# A IS FOR AMANDA

*I was twenty-two when I met my wife, Amanda. That was the best day of my life. She is my guiding star, always has been, always will be.*

*We've been through a lot together, most of it my fault. So when I saw the article in* Somerley News, *I thought it was the perfect opportunity for me to say thank you to her and, well, sorry for having to put up with so much from me.*

*I'm a recovering alcoholic. Amanda helped me through the years that I wasn't myself. If you've never had an addiction, you won't understand the draw towards something you can't have because it's poisonous to you. I'm not making excuses for myself because it was me who started to drink heavily. But I put my family through so much and I'm grateful that I have come out the other side.*

*We don't have alcohol in the house anymore. When we go out with friends, they know not to badger me to join in with them. Besides, there are some great non-alcoholic drinks on the market now. I wish they'd been available years ago.*

*At my lowest, I was a bloated, drunken, snivelling mess. It if wasn't for Amanda, I honestly don't know if I'd be here to write this letter. I was out of control. I'd end up in a fight at the pub; I'd trip over while walking home and end up for hours in A&E. I've narrowly missed being run over several times as I've staggered into the road. I've even passed out and slept in someone's front garden in the middle of winter.*

*And that was outside. In the home, I've fallen down the stairs several times, breaking many bones in the process.*

*I've lost job after job when I haven't been able to do the work I was paid to do. Some days I simply never turned up. I must have been hell to live with.*

*Yet, through it all, Amanda was glued to my side. I honestly don't know why. But she's always said she married me for better and for worse and, even though the worse part has been longer than she'd hoped, she could always see better times emerging.*

*She was right. I've been sober now for two years. It was really hard at first, and I lapsed three times, but eventually, I swapped alcohol for other things.*

*Spending time with my children, not falling asleep or slurring at them.*

*Going on holiday with my beautiful wife and enjoying the area rather than only seeing the inside of the nearest bar.*

*Jumping out of bed in the mornings, not clutching my head as it pounded.*

*Like I say, I don't really know how she put up with me, but I am truly grateful that she did. The best day in my life was when I met her. Thanks, Amanda, for being my rock.*

*John Trevors*

# CHAPTER TWENTY-TWO

Eve was excited about meeting Mack that evening. She put on a dress, dismissed it quickly, and shrugged out of it. She tried another – no, she didn't like that either.

She rummaged around until she found the perfect thing, a denim shirt dress buttoned up its front. Yes, that was the one. It made her feel sophisticated and trendy at the same time. She teamed it with navy ankle boots, and she was ready.

Mack's flat was in a new-build block of four, on the first floor. She found an allocated space and parked the car. Then she sat for a moment to steady her nerves. All the build-up over the past couple of weeks had been leading up to tonight. She had a feeling it was going to be the one that moved their relationship on.

After the party at Somerley Heights, Mack had been constantly on her mind. What she'd had with him had been special when they were teenagers, but she knew those kinds of memories often get contorted through the years. Yet, maybe it was because he was her first love that she felt as if she was being given another chance. Not just to be with Mack, but also to be part of a couple again.

She rang his doorbell and, with a quick hello, he buzzed her in through the communal door. Upstairs, he was waiting for her in his doorway, looking all suave and sexy in a crisp white shirt and sand-coloured jeans.

Kissing her on the cheek in greeting, he beckoned her inside. 'You're here at last.'

'Oh, am I late?' Eve checked her watch to see that she wasn't.

'No, I've just been counting down the minutes.' He smiled sheepishly. 'I couldn't wait to see you.'

It was obvious from the moment she stepped into Mack's home that there was more than food on the menu. She found herself in his arms, pressed against the wall as he kissed her with a passion that she hadn't experienced in a long time. Coming up for air, she gave him a sultry smile.

'That was a nice welcome.' *And hopefully a taste of what was to come.*

'Come on, let's eat.' He took her by the hand and led her through to the kitchen.

'Are you trying to outdo me?' She pointed to the table, set out to restaurant standards. There was even red roses in a vase to one side.

'I wanted it to be special.' He drew out a chair for her.

'Any reason why?' she asked as she settled in her seat.

'Nothing more than it's so great to spend time with you.'

Dinner was lovely, and before long they moved through to the living room, where they sat next to each other on the settee. The room had a warm feel to it, all shades of purple and grey, but not at all masculine.

Eve took the photos from her bag, and they shared a pleasant few minutes going through them, reminiscing. When she came to the photo that she'd got out of the envelope first, she pointed to one of the boys.

'See him? Paddy Stapleton. I Googled him, he lives in

Australia now. He's the head of a big pharmaceutical company.'

'Really? Wow, I never expected that.'

'Me neither. He was such a joker, and he barely concentrated in class. Maybe that's why. Perhaps he was a child genius and therefore bored.'

'Well, monotony was one of the worst things about school.' Mack screwed up his face. 'I don't know how anyone remembers that era of their life fondly. I used to get picked on by Davy Malcolm and his merry men of bullies all the time. It got so bad that I skipped the last month of school, and only went in for my exams, and the last day for the leaving party.'

'That's right.' Eve nodded. 'I kept looking for you and I couldn't find you. Dave really was a twerp. He works at the petrol station now, you know.'

'I doubt he'll even recall the episode.'

'Most people change as they grow older, don't they?'

'Not all of them.' He glanced at her shyly. 'I think I still have a crush on you from nineteen eighty-five. When you had blonde streaks in your hair, and you wore electric-blue mascara. When you were wearing stonewashed skinny jeans and those tight ribbed vests under a denim shirt. When you clattered about in a pair of heels that one of your friends lent to you when you got out of your house for the evening.'

'Stop it, you.' Eve slapped his hand playfully, although she remembered a version of him that was very similar. He always wore skinny jeans, checked shirts with white T-shirts underneath, his hair with messy spikes, and there was always that cheeky grin.

'I mean it,' Mack continued. 'I haven't felt this happy in a good while since you and I reconnected. It's made me realise what I've been missing.'

Eve blushed. The atmosphere in the room was intensifying and, frightened of her gathering emotions, she showed him the note.

'I also found this. I didn't even know I still had it, to be honest. It was tucked in with the photos.'

She waited while he read it, watching him intently.

His face dropped. 'Wow, I hadn't remembered sending that. Was that really how I ended things between us?'

'Yes, and no. You never came home at half-term, and I got one day with you that Christmas. An afternoon really, and then you went back to uni and called it off a couple of weeks later.'

'I'm sorry.'

'Don't be. You were in Lancashire, and I was here. It couldn't have been much of a relationship.'

'You're making me feel terrible,' he protested.

'I meant to!' She took the letter from him and popped it back into the envelope. 'Because you broke my eighteen-year-old heart.'

Mack was mortified. He clearly hadn't realised she was pulling his leg. She laughed at his expression.

'We were teenagers,' she explained. 'I'm not sure anyone knows what love is at that age.'

He stared at her then, the heat in her rising at its intensity.

'Would you like to stay the night?' His voice was husky with emotion.

'Yes, I think I'd like that.' She gave her answer without a second thought. 'I'd better let Grace know I won't be home.'

'Ah, the perils of dating when you're older. Telling your kids you're staying out for the night.' He laughed. 'Mind you, I'm as nervous as hell. I'll pour more wine.'

Eve sent the message to Grace.

*Staying over at Mack's tonight. Don't wait up.*

A reply came back instantly.

*Wait, there's been kissing already?*'

Eve smirked as she replied.

*Just a few times.*

*You dirty cat! Seriously, have fun. Oh, and don't forget to take precautions.*

Eve snorted at that.

'What's so funny?' Mack asked, coming in with two full glasses.

She showed him the messages, and he smiled. 'She's great, your Grace.'

'Never mind Grace. I think we should practice that kissing thing again.'

Eve woke up the next morning, smiling when she realised where she was. She turned to see Mack lying beside her. Gorgeous, sexy man. What a night she'd had.

She'd been right about the sex. After overcoming her nerves, lust had come naturally. It had been wonderful to be aroused and woken up again after so long with a touch of a hand, a lick of a tongue, a gentle bite of teeth. Lips everywhere, bodies joined. It was... she smiled again. It was good to feel so alive.

'Morning.' Mack opened his eyes. He place a hand on her thigh. 'I wasn't dreaming then.'

'No, you weren't.'

'Glad to see you still here.'

'Where did you think I'd be?'

'Perhaps back at home regretting a one-night stand?'

He was teasing her, so she joined in. 'So that's all I'm good enough for, the one night?'

'I bloody hope not.' He pulled her into his arms. 'Do you have plans for today?'

'Cleaning. Ironing. Food shopping. Oh, the glamour.'

'Nothing that can't wait, I see. How about breakfast in town and then a walk around Sapphire Lake? I haven't been there in years.'

'You won't believe how much it's changed.'

'Sounds like a plan, then. Well, obviously not straight-away.' He ran a finger down her arm, causing her to shiver.

It was three-thirty by the time he dropped her off at home after a wonderful time.

Grace was in the kitchen, sitting at the table. 'Afternoon,' she said, her eyebrows raised. 'I take it you had a nice time?'

'I did.' A rush of heat came over Eve when she thought about it.

'You look so happy, Mum.' Grace squeezed her hand as she passed by on the way to the kettle. 'It's great to see you smiling again.'

'Thanks, love. It's nice to have something to smile about!'

## CHAPTER TWENTY-THREE

Grace was at her desk, going through that morning's letters. There had been some great ones coming in lately, and she had a pile to choose from for that week's two-page spread. Even so, she opened them with trepidation, hoping not to receive another poison pen note.

It had been a week since the letter had been delivered, and she was hoping because she'd ignored it that it would be a one-off. Still, after her run-in with Liam, she wondered if it was him even though he'd denied it, twice now.

Flora was sorting out her filing before heading to reception. 'What have you got going in the paper this week, Grace?' she piped up from the seat next to hers.

'I've had several days with best friends, parents, and siblings coming in, so I thought I'd use some of those. Add a bit of light-heartedness after some of the sombre ones. There's also one about a man who helped mend a woman's washing machine and then became her husband a year later. I like those best, really. The odd chance meeting that turns into something.'

'Like you and Tyler, you mean?' Flora eyed her with suspicion.

'What?'

'Although I have to admit, yours are not exactly by chance. You practically stalk him each morning.'

'Can't a woman have a male friend without everyone jumping to conclusions?'

'Yes, of course, but not every one of those women would probably blush as much as you do when he arrives, nor dive into the ladies to freshen up even though you've only been at work for half an hour.'

Flora stared at her pointedly, causing Grace to laugh.

'A girl has to look her best at all times.' She smirked.

'You should write him a letter.'

'And say what?'

'That you—'

'Could I have everyone in the board room for a moment, please?' Tom shouted from his office.

Grace and Flora glanced at each other. Joe wasn't in yet, and Della was just shooting through the doors in the nick of time.

'What's going on?' she asked, removing her jacket. 'Where's everyone going?'

'Tom wants a word with us all,' Grace told her.

'I hope it isn't more redundancies,' Ethan remarked. 'I'm about to apply for a mortgage.'

'You're moving out of Hope Street?' Flora remarked. 'I never thought I'd see the day.'

'Need a bigger place, with a garden.'

'It won't be anything as drastic as job losses,' Grace humoured. Then, 'Will it?'

Once they were in the room, Tom spoke. 'I've just had a call from Joe's wife, Fiona. Joe had a heart attack this morning.

He's been taken to hospital and is being kept in while they monitor him. Fiona says it's not touch and go, but until they get to the bottom of it, he could be in grave danger of having another one. He's having lots of tests today to figure out why.'

Silence dropped on the room as they all took in the news. Some of them would have been feeling guilty about their own selfish thoughts before they'd come in the room. Their jobs were safe. Their working team was not.

Then, except for Grace, they all spoke at once.

Tom raised a hand for quiet. 'Flora, can you order some flowers? Perhaps a basket of fruit or whatever, too. Get it sent here, please, and I'll take it myself.'

Flora nodded.

Grace shook her head in disbelief. 'He seemed fine yesterday,' she spoke quietly.

'Heart attacks can be so sudden,' Ethan replied. 'No time to do anything to stop them a lot of the time.'

'Yes, I know, only too well!'

Ethan's face creased up in horror when he realised his mistake. 'Oh, I'm sorry, Grace, I didn't think.'

Grace scraped back her chair and fled from the room. She hid in the ladies' while she tried to calm down. Tears poured down her face, but she wasn't quite sure who they were for. For Joe, for herself, or if this was about her dad.

This couldn't be happening.

Grace had never forgiven herself for being out on the night her dad had died. She was certain she wouldn't have been able to save him, but nevertheless, it felt like a betrayal not to have been with him.

She recalled the phone call from her mum asking her to come home. She'd said Clark wasn't well but hadn't told her that he'd died until she'd got there. At first, Grace had been angry that she'd lied to her. It was only later she'd realised how her mum had wanted to tell her the news face to face, so that she could comfort her immediately.

The house had felt so empty without him for quite some time. Grace had been living with Liam then. She'd worried about her mum, said she'd come home for a while, but Eve was adamant she'd be okay.

Grace had to abide by her wishes, even though she hadn't wanted to. It didn't seem right to leave her mum alone. But Rose had stepped in for a few nights, until Eve had told her to leave, too.

After the initial shock had worn off, Grace was feeling a little calmer and went back to her desk. Tom immediately came over to her.

'Why don't you work from home today? Della can hold the fort here.'

The look Della threw Tom said she could do no such thing. 'Well, there's a lot of tasks that need completing, and I—'

Tom ignored her protests. 'Excellent, that's sorted then.'

For once, Grace didn't take any satisfaction in Della being put in her place.

'I'd like that, thanks.'

Perhaps she'd catch her mum at home. She'd got a message from her just after going in to the meeting room. She would be heading to the hospital to comfort Fiona soon.

Grace reached for the bundle of letters that had come in since yesterday but had yet to be opened. 'I'll take these with me and read through them this afternoon.'

'You don't need to do that,' Tom said.

'I'd like to.'

Eve was in the kitchen when Grace arrived home. Grace could tell she'd been crying, and the sight of it made her burst into tears, too. She rushed into her mum's open arms.

'It's a bit of a shock, isn't it?' Eve said, hugging her tightly.

Grace sensed her mum's grief as she rubbed at her back, the way she had done when she was a child.

'I knew it would upset you, too,' she said.

'Don't worry about me. Would you like to come to the hospital with me? I'd understand if not, but I'd love the company.'

Grace nodded. Fiona would no doubt be distraught. Clark's death had destroyed Eve at the time. She had been so upset, blaming herself for not keeping him alive, yet there was nothing anyone could have done. No one even knew he had a problem. He kept himself fit, running several times a week. He watched what he ate, and he didn't drink much. But then again, how can anyone know if there wasn't a problem they could see?

Now something similar had happened to Joe, Grace realised that he gave her more support than he could ever imagine. He was always there to pick her up, make her laugh when she was feeling down. Always there to praise her when she did something well. Always there with a helping hand, a guiding word or two when she got things wrong.

Grace gave her mum a squeeze before pulling away. 'Tom is sending gifts from us all.'

'I'll pick some flowers up on the way, too.' A message came in on her phone. 'It's Fiona. Joe is more stable now, but there are still tests to run. That's a relief, though.'

Grace nodded, her eyes watering again. She hoped Joe was over the worst of it. She couldn't bear to lose him, too.

# 2003

*My dearest Rose,*

*I hope this finds you well. It finally finds me as a granddad! Boy, those kids of mine made me wait, but in this past decade, we've had five little ones added to our family. I might be sixty now, but they all keep me young. So, in order, here we go.*

*Michael and Katie have twin sons, Matthew and James. They're both eight. We couldn't believe it when they had twins. There are none on either side of each family. Identical ones, too. It's really hard to tell them apart if you don't know their quirks. They often fool us, pretending to be each other.*

*Both Michael and Katie work at the same hospital, so they live quite close to Newcastle. We see them as often as we can. We can also step in to look after the boys at any time now, as Betty has finished work.*

*Rachel and Denton are back from Australia and have settled in Manchester. They have a daughter, Megan, who is nine, and a son, Jack, who is seven. Rachel works at an advertising agency, and Denton has his own accountancy business. Between me and you, I think their marriage isn't working and I'm expecting them to separate soon. It will be sad, but we'll do whatever we can to support them all.*

*Charlotte is married, too, five years ago. Rob is a police officer, and they have Kelsey who is two. She is a little diamond, I can tell you.*

*They all run rings around their grandparents. We spoil them rotten.*

*I've got another few years until I retire permanently. I'm still at the factory, one of their longest employees now. I know lots of people will mock me for staying with the same company for over forty years, but they have taken care of me well, so I had no need to look elsewhere.*

*Betty didn't get to retirement age before she had to leave her job. She's been unwell, breast cancer. She had to have chemotherapy and then a mastectomy and radiotherapy, but she's been clear for two years now. We're keeping everything crossed that it doesn't come back.*

*I'm in good health, to be honest. I keep myself fit by walking along the lanes, and I've never been a big drinker, nor have I ever smoked, plus I watch what I eat.*

*All this makes me sound like a saint, doesn't it, Rose? I do have my horrible moments, Betty will vouch for that, and the kids have got the wrath of me over the years, but I'm not going to tell you all about that. I want to think of the better times, happy memories I made with my wife and family. Because I hope you had the chance to do the same. Granny Rose sounds wonderful to me.*

*All my love,*
*Cedric*

## CHAPTER TWENTY-FOUR

It was close to midnight, and Eve was lying awake in bed. Her mind wouldn't settle after the events of the day. At the hospital, Fiona had broken down in the corridor outside Joe's ward as soon as Eve got her alone. It had been awful to see her friend in so much pain, worry etched on her face.

Afterwards, she'd dropped Grace off at home and gone to visit Mack. He'd known she was coming and had prepared her something to eat. But the normality of being with him brought back vivid memories, and it hadn't felt right, so Eve had left early.

All through the day, as the memories and the pain came flooding back to her, she began to wonder if she could cope with getting close to someone again. With the fear of losing them hanging over her, she had to reconsider if it was a good thing or not. She liked Mack, a lot, and she hadn't dated anyone since Clark's death because there wasn't that pull to do so. But she couldn't stand the thought of going through that angst again.

She recalled Clark's funeral. It had been a lovely summer's day, just like it had been today. She'd stipulated mourners didn't need to wear black, that Clark would prefer bright colours even though they hadn't discussed it. The church had been full of reds and whites, and yellows and blues, pinks and purples. Lots of tears intermingled within the array of colours.

Everyone had gathered at the Hope and Anchor, the wake lasting far longer than she'd anticipated. The funeral had been held at two-thirty, and yet there were still some stragglers in the bar at half past six. Some of them were a little worse for wear, but they all had nice things to say about Clark, and it had been a tonic to hear anecdotes that she hadn't heard before.

She'd left alone, despite Rose's and Grace's protestations. Exhaustion flowed through her, but she'd gone for a walk around the town. She'd ended up in Somerley Park, circling the lake. The night had been warm, and there were lots of people enjoying themselves because of it. Young couples hand in hand or with a child or two in tow. Joggers, bikers, a pair of teenage girls on roller blades. Elderly men congregating around the bowls green. Friends like her and Fiona out for a natter.

She'd been putting off returning to a home that was now a house. To a life of waking up alone, getting through long and painful days without her husband by her side, and trying to sleep each night.

Everything about the house was steeped in life stories. Memories faded but never left entirely. Back then, she'd assumed one day she'd look into each room fondly, remembering something. Thinking of something.

In the kitchen, bickering over whose turn it was to make a cup of tea.

In the living room, either end of the settee watching TV.

In the hall, when they'd moved in and dragged box after box through the house.

In their bedroom, prodding him in the back to turn over because he was snoring louder than a train.

In Grace's bedroom, sitting next to her, arm around her while they read a book together.

In the garden, when they'd almost broke their backs trying to save money by landscaping their own space.

When Clark had passed, Fiona and Joe had been stalwarts for Eve. They'd helped her through lots of dark days and sleepless nights when she hadn't wanted to share her grief with Grace or her mum. It was hard to keep it all hidden – it had to come out occasionally – so it was Fiona's shoulder she'd cried on when she'd tried to adapt to her future without Clark.

Even now she missed him, often expecting him to walk through the front door of an evening, his routine embedded so much in her mind. She still felt married to him somehow: felt disloyal having feelings for Mack.

But she was alive, and that was always a good thing.

A tear dripped down her cheek. Why did what had happened to Joe have to bring back all her pain when she'd been feeling so great lately? Now, it felt as if it was yesterday when Clark had died.

Time didn't really heal the pain. It just made the gap longer since it had happened. People expected you to move on, but until you'd experienced the raw pain of losing a part of you, how would anyone know how long it would be before that happened?

She'd wanted to speak to Clark on the night he'd died, to at least say goodbye, be with him to allay his fears as he'd taken his last breath.

She'd wanted Clark to speak to her. But there hadn't been the opportunity.

That was the worst of it.

So even though it wasn't the same outcome, she knew

how Fiona would be feeling. She'd be terrified Joe would have another heart attack, a fatal one this time. The fear of losing her husband would derail her. But Eve would rally round them both and help as best she could.

It was no good. Maybe a cup of tea might settle her. She pulled back the duvet and crept downstairs.

At the kitchen table, she sipped at her drink. Still thoughts went round and round her head. Could she take a chance with Mack? Or would the pain of losing someone again be too much? It had broken her when Clark had died, but she didn't want to live an empty life now because of it. Even if that meant being scared for the rest of her life.

'Are you okay, Mum?'

Eve turned to see Grace standing in the doorway hiding a yawn.

'Can't settle, so I'm having a brew. Would you like one making?'

'No, I'm going to grab some water. I just saw the light on and came to see how you are. It's been a tough day.'

'I know. Let's hope Joe continues to improve.'

Grace sat across from her, and they chatted for a few minutes. Eventually, they went back to bed. Eve hoped her mind would settle enough for her to at least get a little sleep. Because tomorrow, she had some serious thinking to do.

# D IS FOR DIVORCE

*The best day in my life that I will never forget is when my decree absolute came through. Yes, I know all you romantics out there will think this sounds weird, but hear me out.*

*I was in a coercive and sometimes abusive relationship. I was made to feel as if everything was my fault, that I couldn't do anything right. I was twenty-one when we met and soon completely head over heels in love, because he was so nice to me to gain my trust.*

*Once we were married and I moved in with him, things started to change. At first it was the little things. When I mentioned I was going out with friends, he'd sulk and say he was looking forward to spending a night with me. Then if I still wanted to go out, he'd criticise my clothes, my hair, too much makeup. Anything to undermine my confidence. Yes, everything you hear happening to other people, the warning signs, the triggers, I ignored because I thought it would make things worse.*

*I tried to get away several times. But he'd always find out where I was. I didn't have many friends left, nor places to go. I had no money, no self-esteem, nothing. He left me a shell of my former self.*

*One night, he beat me within an inch of my life. Had it not been for me being able to crawl to the front door and alert my neighbour, I'm not sure whether I would be here to write this letter at all.*

*I fought back, literally in some instances, but he always wore me down.*

*I honestly never thought he'd let me go, but finally, with police intervention, he got the message and left me alone. So now I get to live life the way I want, even though I still have a tendency to look over my shoulder all the time.*

*But I can wear what I want, go out when I want. Hell, I can eat what I want. There is no one to tell me that I am doing something wrong or that I'm stupid. There is no one telling me that I will amount to nothing. And there is no one who can tell me not to go to college and follow my dream to be a designer. Yes, I'm doing something for me, at last.*

*I'm forty-seven. I was married to him for over half my life. Now I'm going to enjoy the rest of it without him. And one day, I hope there will be someone special out there for me. Someone who will treat me the way I should be treated. Love me with all his heart. Make me the centre of his world. That's what I deserve and that's what I will strive for.*

*So for all those people out there in my position, if this letter helps in any way, this is my gift to you. I survived. That was the best day in my life, when it began again.*

*Jane Doe*

## CHAPTER TWENTY-FIVE

Early that morning, Grace was busy going through her emails when one pinged in and made her gasp.

Flora, who was sitting across from her while reception was quiet, popped her head up over the top of her monitor. 'What's up?'

'I've had an email from *BBC News*. They've heard about the project and want to come and film us!'

'That's so exciting! Don't tell Della. This is your project, and she'll want to take over for sure. I know you're a team player, but this really was all down to you.'

'Actually, that's not true,' Grace replied. 'It was my gran's idea. And I think if I'm going to be interviewed on TV about it, then she should be involved, too.'

'I think Rose will be ecstatic to be on camera.' Flora swiped a chocolate digestive from the packet on the desk between them and dunked it in her tea. 'She's such a character.'

'She wasn't always like that. Before my granddad died, Gran was a quiet soul. She would barely leave the house and had no friends of her own. When he died, she stayed the same for a few months and then she joined a couple of groups at the community centre, and I've seen her change completely.'

'Sounds like for the better,' Flora noted.

'Yes, I'm happy she's found some friends. I wouldn't want her to be lonely.'

'What about another man?'

'Oh, no, she'd never tarnish my granddad's memory.'

'She wouldn't be. She'd just be enjoying what she had left of her life.'

'I suppose.' Grace shrugged, not keen on the idea regardless.

'So if your mum started seeing someone seriously, like this Mack she's dating, for instance, you wouldn't like that either?'

'Mum's only fifty-four. She deserves to find someone to love her.'

'But your gran is too old?' Flora scoffed.

'I didn't say that!'

Flora stared at her pointedly. 'It's never too late for love.'

Grace knew when she was beat, so she screwed a piece of paper into a ball and threw it at her. It bounced off Flora's shoulder, and she laughed.

'What are you two up to?' Della asked as she sashayed across the office and sat down at her desk.

Grace glanced at Flora who said nothing. But she had to tell her. There was no way around it.

'Ooh, I'm going to be on TV,' Della squealed afterwards.

'Afraid not, Del.' Flora shook her head. 'It's on Friday, and you'll be sunning yourself in Lanzarote.'

'They can change the date. They must wait until I come back.'

'I'm not sure that's wise. We could miss the slot entirely.' Grace pressed the point. 'You know how quickly the news flows.'

'Give me their phone number, and I'll call them.'

A few minutes later, they heard her finishing her call. 'No, no, it's fine to go ahead as planned. I'm sure my assistant will be fine.'

Grace high-fived Flora quietly before she disappeared to reception, even though she was annoyed Della had downgraded her role. Della might be senior to her, but Grace wasn't her assistant.

Minutes later, Flora was back and had popped more post in Grace's in-tray. The second of today's project letters was another poison pen. It was so annoying, wondering – no, worrying – who could be doing this.

'Do you fancy lunch out, Flora?' she asked.

Away from the office, they each bought a meal deal from Somerley Stores and went to sit under the oak tree in the square.

'I've received another letter.' Grace got it out of her bag and passed it to Flora.

Flora frowned before dipping her head to read.

*Everyone thinks you are sweetness and light, but you are nothing but a bitch.*

Flora gasped, automatically turning the note over to see if there was anything on the back. But it was blank. 'Who would send such a thing? Who would *say* such a thing?' Are you okay?'

'I don't know. I mean, why is this happening to me?' Her eyes brimmed with tears all of a sudden.

'I'm not sure what to think now there's been two.' Flora handed the letter back to her.

'Do you think someone wants me to publish them in the paper, to show negativity towards the project? I never would, but other than that, I can't think what anyone would get out of it.'

'Me neither. A reaction from you, maybe? It could be someone close to you. Are you sure it isn't Liam?'

'After the last time I saw him?' Grace shook her head. 'It's not him.'

'So who could it be then?'

'I don't know. Still, it was a good excuse to catch up with you for lunch.'

Flora gave her a hug. 'Do you think we should do a stakeout?'

'Like they do on detective shows?'

'Yes. I bet someone drops them off before they go to work in the morning. We could get up early, sit and wait in one of our cars, and see who posts it.'

'Couldn't we just check CCTV? It will be so much easier.'

'But not as much fun, and it takes hours.' Flora was all for it. 'We could be *Scott and Bailey*!'

'Who?'

Flora stared in astonishment. 'You don't know who they are?'

'Just kidding.' Grace thought about it for a moment. 'We could try that, I suppose.'

'I think we should. We definitely need to get to the bottom of who it is.'

'Okay, let's do it.' Grace folded up the letter and popped it back in its envelope. 'In the meantime, I'll keep this to myself while we check through CCTV when we can. And I'll tell Gran the news about the TV this evening.'


Grace arrived home just after her gran had got there but waited until they were all seated at the kitchen table before she mentioned anything.

She looked at Rose. 'I have some exciting news for you.'

'What is it, love?' Rose popped a spoon of rice onto her plate.

'I've had an email from *BBC News* today. They want to do a piece to camera about my project!'

'Oh, that's wonderful, Grace,' Rose exclaimed.

'Isn't it just?' Eve beamed. 'I'm so proud of you. Do you know when it's happening?'

'That depends... on you, Gran,' Grace said. 'It was your idea to ask people to write letters, even if the original idea was changed without my knowledge. But you're my inspiration, and I want to tell everyone that. I'd like you to be interviewed, too.'

'It's your project, love.' Rose shook her head. 'Anyone can have an idea. It was you who followed through with it.'

'I won't take no for an answer, Gran. I've run it through with the producer, and she thinks it's a great idea. She says it will give the piece a community spirit feel with family at the heart of it.'

'Do, it, Mum,' Eve said. 'It will be fun.'

'You should come, too,' Rose said to Eve.

'Oh, no.' Eve smiled. 'It's you she wants.'

'Family, she said.'

'Mum?' Grace eyed her inquisitively.

'Thanks, but I think it should be the two of you.'

Rose paused. 'What if I slip up and say something I'm not supposed to?'

'It won't be live.' Grace reassured her. 'They'll probably do a couple of hours filming, with us saying different things, and then they'll piece together a short clip from it all. Please, Gran. I think it would be fun.'

Rose seemed to ponder for a few seconds before nodding. 'Okay, then. I'll do it.'

'Great!'

'You'll have to tell everyone at Somerley Heights when it's

going to be on.' Eve picked up the salt shaker. 'You'll be a celebrity.'

'Only if I do something silly.' Rose giggled. 'Maybe I'll do a Bridget Jones, climb down a fireman's pole and flash my drawers at everyone.'

'Getting you down the pole would be a thing of glory,' Eve chided. 'You'd be aching all over.'

'But I'd be able to have a fireman's lift.'

'Gran, what are you like?' Grace laughed, thinking back to her conversation earlier with Flora. Would she really mind if her gran found love with another man? Would she be happy for her eventually?

Because, no matter what age, everyone needed someone to love.

## CHAPTER TWENTY-SIX

'Yoo-hoo!' Rose shouted, thrusting her hand in the air to wave at Grace.

Grace turned to see her in all her best clobber and smiled when she walked across to her. 'Morning, Gran, you look amazing.'

Rose winked. 'What, in these old things?' She was wearing a lilac dress with a matching jacket, purple kitten heels, and the hugest of grins. The colour of her nails matched her lipstick, and her dark-grey handbag finished it all off perfectly.

Grace smirked. 'Are you excited?'

'A little bit, yes, but a lot more nervous.'

'It will be fun.' Grace leaned in closer. 'I'll let you into a secret. I am, too. But I'm not telling anyone else!'

Rose placed a hand on her granddaughter's face. Grace covered it with her own, feeling Rose's ageing skin beneath her younger fingers. She dreaded the day anything happened to her. Losing her, too, wasn't something she thought about often. It was far too painful.

'Is your mum around?' Rose asked.

'Yes, she's sitting over there.' Grace pointed her out. 'She still won't join in, though. The producer agrees with her actually. She says it's a lovely story of...' Grace stopped before she put her foot in it.

But Rose had a comical expression on her face. 'You were going to say old and young, weren't you? You can say it, I won't be offended. I know I'm decrepit compared to you.' She put a hand to her hair and patted her perfectly styled curls. 'But I've still got it.'

Grace roared with laughter. 'Come on, let me introduce you to Spike.'

'Spike?'

'She's the producer. The one with the—'

'Bright pink spiky haircut by any chance?'

Grace grinned and took her over to meet the crew.

Spike thrust out a hand to greet Rose. 'How lovely to meet you at last. Grace has told me all about you. How this project, which is wonderful by the way, was your idea.'

'Well, it was, and it wasn't. I—'

'Forgive me for interrupting.' Spike held up a hand. 'This is what I want to talk to you about, and if you answer my questions, you might forget to repeat them on film. Let's go and see where the best place for you to sit will be, and then we'll begin. Lovely weather for it.'

Grace's shoulders dropped as Rose walked off with Spike. Truth be told, she was more nervous than her gran. She was already imagining fluffing up her lines to camera. It was one thing to be in print, and she was quite happy to do voiceovers to film, but the thought of thousands of people tuning in to hear her speak was more than a little terrifying.

'Grace! How's it going?'

She saw Tyler approaching and beamed. 'I'm probably about to make the biggest tit of myself, but other than that, it's going absolutely fine.'

'It'll be over before long,' he soothed. 'Why are they doing it outside?'

'So that they can have a crowd of gawpers that will put me off,' she muttered. 'I said it would be best indoors, but Spike insisted she wanted to show Somerley off, too.'

'Spike?'

'Producer. Pink hair.'

Tyler glanced around and then nodded. 'Ah, gotcha.'

'Ready when you are, Grace!' Spike waved at her.

'Best of luck,' Tyler said.

'Thanks.' She grimaced. 'I may need saving later.'

'How about a quick drink after work?'

'Great, I can tell you all about it then.'

The filming didn't take as long as Grace had anticipated, and it was a joy to do it without having Della breathing down her neck. It was all done and dusted within an hour and a half.

Spike and her crew had gone, Rose, too, and Grace was back at her desk. It had been a surreal day, and although thankful it was over, she was eager to see the finished clip of film. It would be going on the evening news tomorrow if it was good to go by then.

'How did it go?' Tom stopped at her desk. 'Ethan said it seemed like you were a natural on camera.'

'That's because I spent most of last night holding a hairbrush as a microphone in the mirror, talking to myself while I went through all the possible questions I might be asked.'

Tom laughed. 'I hope it was worth it. Sometimes I find the more I practice something, the less natural it comes out at the event.'

'Now you tell me,' Grace wailed. 'I'm doomed.'

'I'm sure you'll be fine. And if it gives the paper, and your project, a boost, then it's worth it.'

. . .

It was just after five-thirty when Eve drove through the gates of Somerley Cemetery. Autumn flowers were in bloom, and it wouldn't be long before the rustic oranges and yellows of the leaves would be colouring the ground.

It was quiet when she got out of her car. She could only see one other person at the far end of a row of graves as she made her way to the garden of remembrance.

At his wishes, Clark had been cremated, his ashes scattered there. Luckily, they'd discussed some things about the eventualities of their deaths before he'd had his heart attack. Eve wanted to be cremated, too, but not for a long time yet, she hoped.

She sat down on a bench, the sun dipping behind a cloud. A breeze blew across the open lawn, and she smiled. Was that Clark, telling her to buck her ideas up, she wondered? Well, it was his fault she felt so wretched, because she still hadn't made up her mind about Mack because of him. That was why she'd come to visit the garden of remembrance.

Eve knew Clark and Mack would have liked each other if they'd had the chance to meet. They were quite similar in their ways, features, too. Like Clark, Mack occasionally wore glasses, to read and when he was driving. Like Clark, he had a great sense of humour.

Like Clark, Mack made her happy.

Was she in love with him already? She suspected so. Yet she was scared of that, too. Mack had probably come into her life at the right time, and here she was, thinking of pushing him away because she couldn't bear to lose him if anything happened to him.

She sighed, her face up to the sky. 'What shall I do, Clark?' she spoke quietly. 'Should I take a chance with Mack? Would you forgive me if I wanted to?'

She contemplated for a while before getting up to go back to the car. But at the last minute she went further into the cemetery. Her father was buried at the back. She didn't visit often now but she remembered exactly where he was.

Standing in front of his grave, she glanced down at the inscription.

*Harold Pritchard. Loving husband and father.*

Well, that was a lie. She huffed. There had been no love in his body. He'd made her and her mum's lives hell on earth at times, ruling the house with an iron rod. And she loathed him for it.

Being brought up in such a fearful environment had meant she'd missed out on so much in life. Harry had always ridiculed any inkling of ambition that Eve had spoken about. Pressed it down, making her feel as if she wasn't capable of anything but mediocracy.

Yet in the end, it was because of her mum that she hadn't ventured out of Somerley. If she'd left, then Rose would have got the brunt of everything. Eve wouldn't wish that on her worst enemy. Harry when he was sober was just about bearable. Harry when he was drunk, coming in from the pub, was a different matter.

Over the years, she'd seen him getting worse. Poor Rose. She'd had no life until he'd died. How cruel was that?

It was in that moment Eve made up her mind. She couldn't live with ifs and buts and maybes. Like Rose, she would miss out on so much if she did. Life was for grabbing, each day precious.

So Eve was going to make sure she was the happiest she could be.

## 2013

*My dearest Rose,*

*How are you doing? As I've kept you up to date with my family, I thought I'd go with the most important thing first. Things have drastically changed in my life. Betty died last year.*

*The cancer came back. Twice she managed to recover from it, but the third time was too much for her to bear. She died March seventh. We were all present when she passed. The whole family around her bed as she took her last breath. I know she would have loved that.*

*I've been at a loss what to do now, to be honest. It's strange when you've had a partner for so long and now they aren't there.*

*It's terrible to lose someone that you've shared most of your life with. I wouldn't wish it upon anyone. But as I'm on my own now, I often think of you. We have been blessed, Rose. I only hope you have been, too.*

*Before she died, Betty told me she'd found my stash of letters to you. I was mortified, but she said she was glad I'd left you behind. Not in a bad way, but she said if I'd stayed in Somerley, she wouldn't have had such a wonderful life with me.*

*Anyway, she told me that one day, I should return to my hometown and find you. I might do that, but not yet.*

*To be honest, writing these letters has kept me close to you. I can't explain why I wanted to do it, apart from the fact that you were always the one who got away.*

*Betty and I had a wonderful life together. I am so grateful for that. But every now and then, especially now, I wonder how different things could have been.*

*Would I swap the life I've had? Not a chance. Would I want to live it again, with you? Yes. But that's just selfish, and impossible.*

*So, instead, I will think of Betty with such fond memories as my heart breaks each night. And every day, on my birthday, Rose, I will think of you, of what might have been. Of what wasn't meant to be. But of what probably made me a better man for Betty as I know I treated her the best I could, to stop her from thinking she was my second choice.*

*My family are growing so fast now. I don't see them as much as I'd like, they're all off doing their separate things. But they all come and see me whenever they can. I'm so grateful to have them around me.*

*I'm thinking of selling up now, though. It's too lonely out here in the sticks. I might move closer to the city again. Newcastle will always be my home. I didn't come here through choice, but it was the right decision in the end. I am grateful for the opportunities I've had.*

*Then again, I might venture back to Somerley. Who knows if it's time for us to meet again? I know you're still alive, Rose. I can feel it in my heart. You nestled there and refused to budge.*

*All my love,*
*Cedric*

## CHAPTER TWENTY-SEVEN

Della pushed her sunglasses down from her forehead, the bright glare of the Spanish sun too much for her as she made her way down to the pool. It was ten-thirty and already twenty-three degrees, without a cloud in the sky. It was also her last full day on the island.

After the first rush of euphoria once she'd made the booking, guilt had shrouded her for several days. She was glad it hadn't been months in advance or she would have cancelled it, but as she'd paid in full, it made her determined to go through with it.

She'd been a bit apprehensive about holidaying as a single, but so far it had been a great experience. The resort was busy enough not to be intrusive, and quiet in places, so she felt safe when she wandered down to the harbour in the evenings.

She spied an empty bed and waved at a woman sitting across the other side of the pool. The woman waved back before her head was immersed in her book again. It was how they'd started up a conversation the other day. It was an LJ Ross detective novel, and Della, having read one or two in the series, found herself in neutral territory for a discussion.

Since then, some of the couples around the pool, and then in the hotel bar, had taken her under their wing. They'd included her in a few nights out, which was kind of them as it was their break, too. Another group had taken her to a casino, where she'd won one hundred euros and had a great night drinking a little too much Sangria.

It made her sad to be on her own, though, although she shuddered inwardly when she thought about her last partner and how she'd treated him. She'd been with Matt for nearly a year. He'd been nothing but loving, kind, and loyal, and yet she'd been possessive, obsessive, and very much the opposite of what anyone would want.

She hadn't been able to tell him at the time that it was down to the relationship she'd had before they'd met. Della had been with Jacob Lucas for a year when she'd found out he was cheating on her, and she'd taken it badly. So much so, that when she and Matt got together, she ruined what they'd had because of her suspicious and ludicrous behaviour. She shuddered, thinking of how it had ended and even then she'd refused to give up for a while.

Now, she was ready to try again with someone new, but there would be no time for the foreseeable future. She was needed at home every evening, and at weekends, there were so many chores to do as well as watching over Mum. It pained her to think that her own life was on hold at the minute, but she had to do what was best.

It was easier when she wasn't alone, though, not to think about home and how her mum would be faring. Chris had been ringing her constantly, at least three times a day, asking if Marianne would eat a certain kind of food or how she liked her tea. What time she went to bed, why she would eat toast one day and hate it the next, not to mention telling her she kept wandering from the guest room all the time.

Lying back on the sunbed, the umbrella up and shielding

her skin from the full heat of the day, she let out a contented sigh. She was going to enjoy the last day of her holiday without guilt creeping up, like it had every second she'd been on the island.

Yet, there was something else on her mind, too. Those notes that she'd left in Grace's in-tray. The more she thought about them, the more she realised how stupid she'd been. And for what? A bit of attention? A reaction? Spite because Grace was so well-liked? It had been childish, and a sackable offence if she'd thought through her actions.

With Grace not mentioning anything to her about either of them, she was thinking that perhaps there was a way of getting them back. She wasn't going to send any more, so if she could find and destroy the letters, then if it was brought up and linked to her, she could deny it. Either that, or she could mention it to Grace, own up and apologise, and see if she would keep it between the two of them. Grace was young, she might not want to do that, but it was worth trying.

Yes, she would get them back once she got home.

# CHAPTER TWENTY-EIGHT

Grace was sitting in her car outside *Somerley News*, with her eyes firmly on the entrance. Flora had cried off their stakeout when she realised how early they would have to start, so Grace had managed to rope Tyler into having a day off in return for taking him out for dinner. It also gave her an excuse to spend more time with him.

He knocked on the window, making her jump.

'What time of the morning do you call this?' Grace asked. 'How on earth do you manage to get up so early every day?'

'Habit now,' Tyler replied, jumping into the passenger seat. 'I have to be at work for half past five if I'm delivering by foot, half six if I'm in a van.'

'Half five?' Grace shook her head. 'I couldn't manage that.'

'You did today.' It was just before six.

'That's because we have an important mission.' Grace pointed to the glove compartment. 'There's provisions for us in there.'

Tyler reached for them, a smile on his face. Biscuits, fruit, and a couple of chocolate bars. 'Nice.'

'There's coffee in a flask, too. I'll need that to keep me awake.'

'The last girl I went out with, Kirstie, said I sent her to sleep with my incessant rattle.'

Grace smirked. She wasn't about to tell him that she was happy his ex was no longer around and that Tyler was single. She'd realised she was looking forward to his daily visits to reception much more than she should be if she didn't have feelings for him. It seemed he was creeping under her skin.

Plus, she also knew he didn't need to drop the letters off. The office wasn't on his route every week, but he made a special delivery to get them to her personally.

She glanced over at him while he opened the biscuits. She usually preferred blonds to darks, but his height over six foot was something she did like. Along with his blue twinkling eyes, smiling eyes.

'Jammie Dodger?' Tyler waved the packet in front of her nose. 'Did you know these are my favourite ever biscuit?'

'Not even a lucky guess. They're just my favourites, too. Are you keeping an eye on the door or are you too busy stuffing your face?' Grace teased.

'Oh, I'm watching. I can multi-task, you know. Hey, did you see that documentary last night? The one about the woman who was murdered by her husband?'

'I don't like true crime. I have an overactive mind and end up having nightmares.'

Tyler paused. 'So why do you have no one to cuddle up to in bed when you're frightened?'

Grace shrugged. 'After Liam's pettiness, I think I prefer to stretch out in a bed on my own.'

'How long were you with him?'

'Four years. He accused me of putting my job before him; can you imagine how childish he sounded?'

'So what was his problem?'

'He didn't like me working during the evenings. It was as if he was jealous of the attention I got. And woe betide anyone who stopped on the street when they recognised me. He'd walk off in a huff and wait for me up ahead.' She grinned. 'I used to make him wait because it annoyed me so much.'

'Yeah, I get that, too, when I'm out. Sometimes I can never get away from the old biddies on the high street.' He paused. 'So there were no plans to marry or have kids?'

'I thought there might have been at first. But even though I was upset when we split, I'm relieved there was nothing more permanent than packing a case and not paying any more rent. I'm not tied to him now. How about you?'

'One relationship very much like yours, petering out when neither of us wanted to commit. But, like you, I expect, I would have if she'd wanted to.'

'She, as in Kirstie?'

Tyler cringed. 'God, no, she was quite the bunny boiler. I only dated her for a few weeks. She was very intense.'

'In what way?'

'Extremely possessive. She was always dropping around every evening. It was okay at first, but then I wanted a night out with friends, and that was when she accused me of not loving her enough. To be fair, I hadn't got to the love stage.'

'Blimey, that does sound intense.'

'Don't get me wrong, I liked her, and she was good company when we were together, but that's *all* she wanted to do. She didn't want to meet my family, nor my friends, and when she found out my best friend was a woman? She almost blew her top.' Tyler shuddered at the memory. 'Clara, that's my friend, works at Wilshaw's Estate Agents, and I've known her since I was a child. We'll never be anything more than friends, but Kirstie wasn't having any of it. She told me it was her or Clara. I've been in this position before, so I told her to sling her hook.'

'I know Clara. She's really nice. I don't blame you for not putting up with that behaviour.'

'So it wouldn't bother you if my best friend was a woman?'

'No, why should it? Couples need friends outside their relationships.' She paused. 'Why do you ask?'

'Oh, nothing. I just wondered.'

She smiled to herself. Was he testing her there, because if so, she had given him the right answer. She wasn't the jealous type, and from what she'd seen of Tyler, being his friend, too, she could imagine him getting on with lots of people.

Something caught her eye.

'Hey, there's someone going towards *Somerley News*.' Grace pointed at a woman. She was wearing a navy-blue skirt suit and a white blouse, black high heels. Her hair was blonde and wavy. At the door, she pulled an envelope from her bag and pushed it into the letter box by the side of the entrance.

'I don't believe this.' Tyler opened the car door.

Grace raced after him, finding it hard to keep up with his long strides.

The woman was coming back towards them now. She stopped as she saw them both approaching her.

'I might have known this would be a trick you'd pull,' Tyler seethed. 'Just what the hell is your game?'

'Get out of my way,' the woman snapped. 'Besides, I don't have anything to say to you anymore.'

'Maybe not.' Tyler grabbed her arm as she tried to push past him. 'But I do think you have some explaining to do, Kirstie.'

*Kirstie?*

Grace's mouth fell open. Was this the jealous ex-girlfriend? That would make sense if she'd seen her with Tyler and thought they were more than friends.

'Take your hands off me,' Kirstie screeched.

Tyler backed off immediately. 'Calm down,' he said. 'It's not as if I'm hurting you.'

'No, you've already done that.'

'I never touched you!' Tyler's eyes widened in distress.

'I meant that you broke my heart.'

'That's different.'

'No it isn't.'

'Look, whatever's been going on between you two,' Grace interrupted their squabble, 'I'd prefer to stay out of it. If it was you who sent the nasty letters, Kirstie, then I think it's mean, and it needs to stop. I don't want—'

'What letters? I've only posted one today.'

'Yeah, right,' Tyler scoffed.

'If you must know, my granddad has written a letter about my late gran.'

'Oh.'

*Oh, no.* Grace watched as Tyler paled.

'I'm so sorry,' Tyler went on. 'I thought—'

'You thought I'd send nasty letters to get back at you? How childish do you think I am?'

Tyler hung his head.

'Why would I do that to someone I don't even know?' She glared at him and then looked at Grace with a frown. 'Wait, you're an item? And you thought I did it out of spite?'

'Oh, no, we're not—' Grace started.

Kirstie ignored her, turning back to Tyler, pointing a finger in his face. 'You and I were over a long time ago. If you think I'd pull a stunt like this, then...' Her voice broke. 'Then good riddance, is all I can say.'

'Kirstie, I'm sorry.' Tyler reached for her arm again, but this time she marched away. 'Ah, come on, it was a genuine mistake.'

Grace stood rooted to the spot, unsure what to do. Tyler's

face was a picture of embarrassment. She tried to contain a nervous burst of laughter threatening to erupt. Poor Tyler.

But then she realised that they were no further forward finding out who the real culprit was. And there was no way she would suggest another stakeout.

# CHAPTER TWENTY-NINE

Rose was on her way down the stairs to the communal lounge, not one to take the lift unless her arthritis was playing up. Grace had rung to say the clip they'd filmed was being shown on tonight's news at tea time. How exciting!

Word had spread like wildfire around Somerley Heights, and she was in no doubt there would be a crowd waiting to watch it with her. But even knowing that, she jumped as she opened the door and a cheer rang out around the room.

'Here she is, the lady of the moment,' Arthur, from flat seven, cried. 'At last. We've been waiting ages for you.'

'I'm here now.' Rose, coming over shy as all eyes fell on her, she searched out Iris who had saved a seat for her in their favourite spot.

'Come on, it's nearly time,' Iris said.

Rose sat down next to her. 'It might not be on at the start of the programme.'

'It won't hurt to watch from the beginning just in case.' Iris picked up two glasses of wine and handed one to Rose. 'Here's to you, Rose Pritchard. The first person in Somerley Heights to get on the telly.'

'You don't know if that's true.' Rose giggled.

'I'd bet my life on it. Nothing this exciting has happened around here before.'

'Shush or you'll miss it,' Herbert from flat two said, urging them to pipe down.

'He hasn't got his specs on, so I doubt he'll see it when it does come on.' Iris harrumphed. 'Nor will he be able to hear it properly.'

Rose nudged her friend, and they laughed like two schoolchildren. A stern look from Herbert, and they shut up, stifling giggles instead.

'It's on, it's on!' Margaret, from flat eight, said. 'Everyone be quiet.'

'I like her, whatsherface, reading the news.' Edward pulled one knee over the other in his attempt to get a little more comfortable. 'Reminds me of my Celia when she was in her heyday, God rest her soul.'

'Shush.' Arthur rolled his eyes.

*'When feature writer, Grace Warrington, needed to come up with a community project for work, she turned to the first person she could think of to help her out. Her gran, Rose Pritchard, came to her rescue. Tell me more about it, ladies. Let's start with Grace.'*

Everyone whooped when there was a close up of Rose and Grace, sitting under the oak tree in Somerley Square.

'The weather was glorious,' Edward commented. 'But not nearly as lovely as you.'

'Oh, give over.' Rose hid her face with her hands for a moment, but then peeped through her fingers. "*What made you ask your gran for advice?*" she heard the presenter ask Grace.

'Has that woman got pink hair?' Margaret shouted loudly.

'Her name is Spike, and she is ever so nice,' Rose replied.

'*Shush.*' Arthur turned to her.

'I'm just saying.' Margaret was put off by his tone. 'It's a bit weird, pink, isn't it?'

'For the love of... please be quiet,' Arthur demanded. 'We're going to miss it at this rate.'

On-screen, Spike was talking to Rose now.

Off-screen, Rose sat quietly, almost in shock. It was so weird seeing herself on TV. But the more she listened to the clip, the more she realised she didn't sound that bad. And she looked rather well, she thought. After a few seconds, her hands were away from her face and resting in her lap.

The camera panned around the square, and there was another clip of Somerley high street before she and Grace were on-screen again.

'*What are your hopes for the project, Rose?*' Spike asked.

'Ooh, your turn again,' Iris chortled, ignoring all the shushes she received.

'*I would love people to join in and share a bit of positivity,*' Rose said. '*The world has been a dark place lately. Everyone could do with cheering up, and there's nothing better than sharing stories about the things in life that really matter to us.*'

Spike nodded, and then the screen cut back to her as she rounded off the piece.

'*So there you have it, folks. If you have something that you'd like to share that would make other people smile, or indeed make someone feel special, the details to enter are on our website and at the bottom of the screen right now. In the meantime, I'm off to find a notepad and pen. I might even enter myself. Sophie Helroy,* BBC News.'

The program returned to the studio as applause went up around the lounge.

'You were great, doll.' Edward winked at her. 'I'd still marry you tomorrow if you'd have me.'

'Get off with you.' Rose tittered.

'I'm sure every man in Somerley will be after you once they see that. You mark my words.'

'He's right, Rose,' Iris concurred. 'You were a natural. Did you tape it so we can watch it again?'

'No one tapes things nowadays,' Herbert admonished. 'I've recorded the program, and it will be shown on catch-up TV, I'm sure.'

Rose didn't say she had recorded it, too. It seemed too modest to own up to that.

'Well, I for one, think it calls for a celebration.' She raised her glass in the air. 'Here's to Grace. I hope you're all going to put together your letters for the project because I want one off you all. I bet we have a lot of best days in our lives to share.'


As he did every week day, Cedric Brownslow took a stroll around the park. He stopped to sit on his favourite bench, overlooking the boathouse and the ducks that congregated on the banks beside the lake.

He chuckled to himself, watching a small girl emptying a bag of bread crusts in one fell swoop instead of throwing them one at a time, and being rushed at by a group of forever hungry birds. She ran into the arms of her mum for reassurance.

Cedric was transported to a time when he and his wife, Betty, had taken their son, Paul, to the park and he'd tripped up in his haste to get to the mallards. Before they could reach him, he'd toppled into the water, and Cedric's heart had almost stopped in his panic to get him out.

He'd dashed in, only to find the water was at the most a few inches deep at that point. Paul had landed on all fours, thankfully with no harm done. Cedric had nightmares about the water being deeper for weeks after that. The perils of life in the seventies when there were less strict health and safety measures.

Back at home, on the stroke of six from the grandfather clock in the hallway, he switched on the TV for the evening news and sat down with a cup of tea and three digestive biscuits. Winnie, next door's cat, who spent more time at his house, jumped up and curled in his lap.

He was about to take a big slurp of his drink when the presenter with the spiky pink hair came into view with two other women. He gasped, putting his mug down immediately.

At first, he thought his old eyes were deceiving him, but then as he leaned forward to look closer, he realised they weren't.

'Is that who I think it is, Winnie?' He reached for the remote control and raised the volume. When the woman with the pink hair said a name from his past, he shook his head in disbelief.

'Well, I never. Rose Machin, as I live and breathe.'

He pressed record and then sat back to watch the rest of the clip.

It really was her.

Hadn't he known she was still alive?

He played the clip over and over, each time his smile widening. Then he pulled himself up from the settee and rooted out a notepad and pen.

# M IS FOR MADGE

*I know you'll probably receive a lot of letters about friends and family for your project, but I wanted to write and tell you about my bestie. It's such a silly word when you're eighty-one, isn't it? But it's true. My bestie has been with me most of my life. And I'd like to thank her. I'm sure she'd be shocked if she saw this letter in the newspaper.*

*We are both avid readers of Somerley News. It's actually more fun for us now it's once a week. That's me and my friend, Madge. We get our copies and we take it in turns to visit each other, the hostess supplying the cakes to go with the tea.*

*We love nothing more than scouring the pages, catching up on the gossip, learning about old friends and reading the news.*

*Madge and I go back years. We met when we were at school and have been inseparable. Between us we've had three husbands and are both widowed now. We share every spare moment that we can together. It's wonderful to have someone to talk to all the time. We reminisce about our youth, talk about our children, and grandchildren, and holidays we've been on. I don't think there has been a week gone by that we haven't met up. We're like two peas in a pod.*

*Madge has been given four months to live. It's okay, she has seen this letter before I sent it to you. So in true best-friend style, we're tackling it together. We're already planning her funeral – it's going to be some party. She wants that to be her best day.*

*I hope she doesn't suffer too much before she goes, but whatever happens, I will be by her side every step of the way.*

*Cybil Hawkins*

# CHAPTER THIRTY

Grace set to work opening the letters that had come in for her project. For the past few mornings, there had been talk and light-hearted leg-pulling about her TV appearance, but now things were starting to calm down. Della had been back in that morning, too, and had rattled for twenty minutes about her trip to the Canary Islands.

There were only two weeks left before the closing date for The One Letter Project. Already, Grace enjoyed the daily ritual of opening that morning's batch and seeing what had come in overnight. She wasn't looking forward to the end date of the competition when there would be no more.

She opened the next one, a smaller envelope falling out, too.

*Dear Ms Warrington,*

*Following your appearance on* BBC News *a couple of evenings ago, I write to you with a query. I wonder if the woman you were with, your grandmother, is someone I used to know by the name of*

*Rose Machin. She may not go by that surname now, of course, but this was her name when I last saw her in 1963, at Kennedy's Factory.*

*If it is, could you pass the enclosed letter on to her, please? I'd be very grateful. I live in hope of an answer, even if it was a long time ago.*

*Yours sincerely,*
*Cedric Brownslow*

Grace frowned as she picked up the other envelope, the name Rose written in shaky handwriting. She turned it over to find it sealed.

She sat back in her chair. 'Oh my.'

'What's the matter?' Della asked.

'Oh, nothing. Just a twinge in my back,' she fibbed, not wanting to share this with her. Quickly, she slid the letter into a manilla file and went to show it to Flora. She found her sorting out the cupboard under the reception desk.

'I've had a letter within a letter,' she spoke excitedly to Flora's bottom.

'Help me up, then.' Flora put out a hand.

Grace pulled her to her feet and passed her the note. She watched eagerly while she read it, waiting for her reaction.

Flora glanced at her, wide-eyed. 'Is this for real?'

'It seems like it,' she said.

'And you think this could be your gran?'

'I don't know but I doubt there's more than one Rose Machin in Somerley.'

Flora pointed at the envelope. 'Where does this Cedric live?'

'Oh, hang on.' Grace looked through the first envelope and letter. 'There's no address, just a Newcastle postmark.'

'Under-Lyme or Upon Tyne?'

'Upon Tyne. Do you think he forgot to put it inside?'

'Well, what's the point of asking you to pass on something and then not giving you details for that person to get in touch? It's a bit crackers, if you ask me.'

'Unless it's inside the sealed envelope.' Grace grimaced. 'What am I going to do with it now? Should I tell Tom? I'm certainly not saying a word to Della. She'll pounce on it for herself, and I'm not sure I'd like that.'

'Yes, I agree. I think you should go and see Rose first.' Flora clapped, excited. 'This might be a love story we could share.'

Grace wasn't convinced. What happened if she raced around to see her gran, then after getting her all excited realised the letter wasn't for her? Grace had never heard her talk of Cedric. Worse, what if it was all a con?

'The least it will do is put your mind at rest,' Flora went on. 'And if it isn't her, we can launch an appeal in this week's paper. To find another Rose Machin, or for Cedric Brownslow to get in touch. You could even contact Spike, do another TV interview.'

Grace thought for a moment. There really was only one way to find out. And if Rose did know Cedric from all those years ago, perhaps she would answer all the questions that were running through her mind right now.

She nodded. 'You're right. I'll go and visit Gran for my lunch and show it to her.'

Once she'd arranged the visit, Grace still couldn't settle. Curiosity coursed through her as she wondered what had been going on. But equally, the journalist in her sensed a story, and she wanted to be the person to break it.


Rose was always delighted to see Grace so had been pleased when she'd rung to ask to come to lunch. She'd finished making sandwiches and slicing cake, the kettle boiled in readiness when Grace knocked and opened the front door.

'Hello, love,' Rose greeted her. 'It's so nice to see you. How are things?'

'They're fine, thanks.' Grace waited until they were both seated. 'I have something to ask you, though. Well, to show you really.'

Rose sat forwards. 'What is it?'

'A letter came to the office this morning. Someone is looking for Rose Machin.'

'But that's me.' Rose frowned.

'The person who wrote the letter wants to contact you. He saw you on the TV with me and—'

'He?'

Grace nodded. 'Cedric Brownslow. He said—'

'Cedric?' Rose's stomach rolled over.

'Why don't you read the letter and see for yourself?' Grace passed it to her.

Heart beating wildly, Rose opened the envelope.

*Dearest Rose,*

*I can clearly remember the day I first set eyes on you. My stomach flipped when you glanced over at me. You were sitting in the work's canteen with two of your friends.*

*I smiled, and you returned it, dipping your eyes in a shy manner that had me sighing. I waited for you to look again, and when you did, this time I kept your gaze.*

*I came to sit with you then. Just for a couple of minutes, can you remember? That's when I lost my heart. I don't think I ever got it back completely.*

*There were circumstances why I left so quickly that I hope I get a chance to explain. Because I never stopped thinking about you.*

*So it was a lovely surprise, as well as a complete shock, to see you*

*on the TV the other evening. You're still as beautiful as ever, and I would love to know how you are.*
*Yours forever,*
*Cedric*

'Well, I never.' Rose put a hand to her chest.

Grace took the letter from her and read it, too. 'Oh, that's so nice.'

'He's someone I used to work with. Cedric left, before I married your granddad.'

'And he hasn't been in contact all these years. Why?'

'I don't know. I've often wondered what happened to him, but it was as if he disappeared into thin air.'

'There's no address, but the post mark is Newcastle upon Tyne.'

Rose reached for the envelope to see for herself. 'So it is. He must have left Somerley to live in Geordie land.'

'So the letter *is* for you?' Grace was flabbergasted.

'I think so. Cedric came to work at the factory, just after I met your granddad. I must admit, I was rather smitten with him. Had he not gone off in such a hurry, I might have married him. He was a wonderful man.'

Rose slipped back to when she had last been with Cedric. He had made her heart sing, her lips crackle at his touch, and she'd been looking forward to meeting him for a proper date.

'Gran?' Grace touched her arm gently.

Rose giggled. 'Oh, I'm sorry, Grace. Getting that letter has taken me back to a time in my life that I was very happy.'

'I still don't understand. Why is he contacting you after all these years?'

'I don't know. Perhaps he was curious when he spotted me on the TV.' She chuckled. 'We've obviously changed. Do you think he wants to meet up with me?'

'Would you like that?'

Rose paused for a millisecond. 'Yes, I think I would.'

Glorious memories flooded back at the way Cedric had made her feel. Rose had always known she'd been more in love with him than she had ever been with Harry. They were only friends back then, but she'd wanted there to be so much more.

## C IS FOR CLEAR OF CANCER!

*Well, what can I say? The best day in my life might not have happened if it wasn't for my GP's surgery, in particular Dr Mia Sharman. You see, I was feeling unwell, and then I found a lump under my arm. There was no waiting for an appointment. I was told to go in that afternoon.*

*Mia examined me, trying not to scare me with her thoughts, not even mentioning the C word, and from that moment on, there was a round of tests over the next two weeks.*

*It was all down to me watching a documentary on the TV about breast cancer. Afterwards, I decided to have a feel around my boobs when I next took a shower. Of course, you're told to do it regularly, and of course you're supposed to do it, but I never really took any notice of that. There was nothing there I could feel, thank goodness, but it made me question why I'd been putting on weight so quickly. I'd also been having trouble with lots of other bodily functions, but we won't go into all that.*

*Sadly, it resulted in something else, my worst nightmare coming true. It was a tumour.*

*The wait for the results had been excruciating, but when I was told, Dr – Mia – sat across from me and my husband to break the news. She was holding my hand and had tears in her eyes. I've often wondered how doctors keep in their emotions when they tell patients something they don't want to hear. I liked those tears, it showed she was human.*

*I was in the hospital a few weeks later having surgery. I'm still recovering from it, if truth be told. But so far, so good. I've since had chemotherapy and done a lot of soul searching, trying to stay positive about things.*

*When I visited Dr Sharman last week, she told me the cancer had been removed completely and that there was nothing there. She wasn't certain it wouldn't come back – she might be superhuman to me, but she hasn't got the powers to see into the future. But for now, I'm ringing that bell when I go for my last chemo next week. And I am starting my life again.*

*You see, all this gave me a kick up the backside. For years, I've wanted to train to be a nurse. Yes, the hours are terrible, and the state of the NHS is, well, let's just say, a lot to be desired. But having a cancer scare made me look at life in a different way.*

*Every day is a gift. We can choose to spend it being miserable, we can choose to spend it being happy. At a flick of a coin, or a mindset switch, I suppose.*

*For me, it's given me time to re-evaluate my life. Put myself first for a change and do something that I thought I'd never do. I may not be cancer-free forever, but I am going to live my life as much as I can until I find out otherwise.*

*Thank you, Dr Sharman, Mia, for giving this patient the best care you could, and the best start to the rest of her life.*

*Teresa Gladden*

# CHAPTER THIRTY-ONE

Grace was quiet when she got back to the office. Flora, who had been on the phone, wrapped up her conversation pretty sharply and rushed over to her. Della was on her lunchbreak, so Flora perched on the end of Grace's desk.

'How did it go?' she wanted to know, keeping her voice low. 'Is it her?'

'Yes, it's her.'

Flora sighed. 'How romantic. Did she tell you how she knew him?'

'Apparently he was someone she met at work while she was with my granddad. She was all for telling him that it was over so she could go out with Cedric. But she panicked and didn't say anything. And when she went to work on Monday, Cedric had left.'

'No way! I have so many questions. Why did he leave? Why didn't he keep in touch? Why didn't he ever return? Has he got family in Somerley that he never visited? This is riveting.' Flora stopped. 'I mean, if Rose is willing to talk about it, obviously. Do you think they'll meet?'

'I don't know. He didn't leave any contact details. Maybe he just wanted Gran to have the letter and nothing more?'

'There's got to be more to it than that. Why now, after all this time?'

'Because he saw her on TV. If he hadn't, he wouldn't have got in touch, would he? I mean, he could easily have come back and searched her out years ago. She wouldn't have been hard to find.'

'I guess so.'

They both looked up when a young woman came into the reception area. Grace followed Flora as she went to deal with her. The woman had a small baby in her arms which they cooed over, and then while Flora dealt with her, Grace sat quietly.

All kinds of emotions were flowing through her. She wanted to be happy for her gran, but it all seemed a bit too much like a fairy tale to her. And what about her granddad and his memories? Would Gran really want to meet another man?

But then, those were all her feelings, and nothing about this situation was up to her to decide what to do next.

Once Flora was free again, they resumed their chat. Grace sighed dramatically. 'The thing is, my gran wants to find him.'

'I knew it!' Flora beamed. 'Good old Rose.'

'She said at her age, you have to take your chances. She said… even though she was married to my granddad, she'd never stopped loving Cedric for all those years.'

Flora mock swooned. 'I think I have something in my eye.'

Grace definitely had tears in hers. The whole thing was upsetting and disrespectful to her granddad who she had loved dearly.

'It's such a lovely story,' Flora added. 'What are you going to do to find him?'

'Well, we could put an article in the paper in the hope he'll see it online.'

'What about getting in touch with Spike and seeing if she wants to do a further piece to camera with Rose, talking about Cedric and how she'd love to see him again? It would get more publicity for the One Letter Project.'

Grace screwed up her face. 'I'm not sure Rose would like all the attention.'

'Are you kidding? She loved being on TV.'

'This is different, though. It's her personal life. There might also be a reason Cedric hasn't come back to Somerley. What if he has family that he doesn't want to know his whereabouts?'

'You have a point. Let's think more social media then. How about our Facebook page? Although, it may catch on, so his family might see anyway.'

Grace was torn. She needed to speak to her mum before doing anything drastic, see what Gran had said to her about it. It wouldn't do any harm to leave it until tomorrow.

'Let's give her time to take it all in.'

They went back to their desks. Flora took a phone call and put it through to Tom before continuing their conversation.

'I think you're right,' she agreed. 'You could be sitting on the biggest love saga Somerley has known, but there's a thin line between a feel-good story and intrusion. I'd hate for us to upset anyone. I'd love to be involved, though.'

Grace nodded. 'It's a deal.' She knew her gran wanted to find Cedric Brownslow, but she had to make sure she realised what may come from it. Perhaps it would be best to leave the past in the past. But that wasn't her decision to make.

Della came marching over, plonking several envelopes into Grace's in-tray. 'More letters for you.'

Flora disappeared again to deal with another customer,

and Grace opened the letters, thankful to see there were no nasty ones for her. She hoped she'd seen the last of them, and the project would be over soon anyway.

She reached into the drawer to retrieve the file where she'd hidden the two she'd received. But when she opened it, there was nothing there. She rummaged through the drawer, wondering if she'd misplaced the letters, but no, they were gone.

She sat back as a horrible thought crossed her mind. Had the letters come from someone in her own team? Had one of them regretted sending them and now wanted to get rid of the evidence altogether?

Which meant someone had been going through her desk.

She looked around the office, at people she had worked with for years. Then her eyes fell on Della. Could it be her?

There was only one way to find out. Grace would choose her time, see if she could start up a conversation when there was just the two of them. She could mention the letters and judge her reaction.

An email pinged in, and she opened it absent-mindedly. But what she read had her mind reeling over what to do next. It was from Cedric Brownslow.

## CHAPTER THIRTY-TWO

It was past nine when Grace got in that evening. Eve had known she was working late at a charity event, so she'd invited Mack for tea. He'd only been gone a few minutes, and she was tidying up in the kitchen.

'You've just missed Mack.' Eve wiped her hands and planted a kiss on Grace's cheek. 'How is everything going?'

'Okay. Me and Flora popped in to see Joe on the way. He's doing well, isn't he?'

'He is. I bet you miss him at work.'

'I feel lost without him.' Grace told Eve. 'I miss Dad so much, Mum. It was like losing him all over again when it happened to Joe, if you don't think that's disrespectful.'

'I know what you mean.' They sat down at the table. 'It really affected me for a couple of days, I must admit. Joe means so much to us, plus all the hurt and pain of losing your dad came back to me. I suppose grief has ebbs and flows. Sometimes I can go for days without thinking of him, and then, bam. I'll hear or see something that reminds me of him and I'm in tears.'

'I didn't know you still felt like that.'

'I can't share every sad moment with you.' Eve smiled kindly. 'What I meant was we grieve in different ways, for different people, *and* for differing lengths of time. The thing is, we can either live a lesser life because of it, or we can embrace what we have in the here and now. It's taken me a long time to realise that it's okay to move on.'

Grace nodded. 'It brought back the suddenness of it to me.'

Eve recalled what Mack had told her about his wife suffering for years. She wouldn't break his confidence by saying anything to Grace, but she could use it as an example.

'Imagine having to watch him suffer, though, if he'd been ill with something which meant he'd faded away over time, and in a lot of pain, like Granddad had been.'

'There is that, I suppose.'

Eve paused, sensing there was something else. She didn't speak, hoping her daughter would bridge the silence. Sure enough, she did.

'Anyway, less about me. I need to talk to you about Gran. I had an email today from Cedric Brownslow.'

'Oh.' When Eve found out about the letter to Rose, she'd been flabbergasted. She and Mack had discussed it, about Eve's feelings if her mum wanted to find Cedric. They'd spoken about her dad, too, and how she didn't give a tuppenny toss about what he'd think. He no longer ruled their lives.

'What did it say?' she asked.

'He was sorry he'd forgot to include his address, so here it was, and that he would love to see Gran if it was possible.'

'What did you do?'

'I rang him.'

'What was he like?'

Grace shrugged a shoulder slightly. 'He seemed nice. He was so grateful I'd called.'

'Oh, that's lovely. Did he say he wants to come and meet her?'

'Yes. Do you think that's wise?'

'I do.' Eve wanted to do things right by her mum. 'I think we should arrange it as a surprise visit. He can come here, rather than us giving out her address. Then we can at least vet him.'

'He sent me this, too.' Grace took out a piece of paper and handed it to Eve. 'It's a photocopy of an old photo, from a work's outing. Gran and Granddad are on it.'

Eve searched out her parents and smiled. Her mum and dad looked so happy, in the throes of first love, she imagined. Before it had all gone wrong.

'That's Cedric, at the end of the first row,' Grace said.

Eve peered at him. He was tall, dark, and even though the image was poor, she could see he had the most incredible smile.

'What did he say when you spoke to him?'

'He wanted to reassure me that he was who he said he was. Maybe he isn't out to dupe an old woman out of her savings after all.'

'Grace,' Eve chastised. 'Email him and see if he'd like to visit one evening, either this week or next. In the meantime, we can keep talking about the letter but put her off contacting him. What do you think? Will that work?'

Grace nodded. 'I think so.'

Eve made fresh tea and then got out the book of photos Grace had bought her the Christmas after Clark had gone. Tea made, they moved to the living room and sat on the settee together.

The first few photos were old ones of the two of them in their early twenties. They followed on with different times in their life: their first home together, a new car, holidays, nights out with friends.

Then Grace had come along, and there were pages of photos of her with her dad, and with them both. Having miscarried before finally carrying Grace to full term, Eve hadn't been in a rush to have a second child. It hadn't happened anyway, and they'd become settled in their team of three.

The photos became less as digital ones had taken over. But Grace had found a few on their phones and added them. The last page was a snap of Grace with Clark. Grace was sitting on his lap like a baby. He was pulling his face as if she was heavy and she was slapping his hand. There had been so much love between them. She had always been proud of the life they'd created for Grace. It had been very different from when Eve was a child, that was for sure.

'Isn't it weird that both you and Gran have found people from your past again?' Grace said. 'I thought it was only my age group that found love. Although, I haven't made a good job of it yet.'

'Your time will come, sweetheart,' Eve responded. 'You wasted four years with Liam – well, three, I suppose. I mostly liked him for the first year.'

'Mostly?'

'Me and your gran had a gut feeling it wouldn't work out in the long term.'

'You never said!'

'Sometimes with love you have to find these things out for yourself. There's nothing truer than love can be blind.'

Grace sniggered. 'At least I have my eyesight back. What about you, though?'

'Me?' Eve knew what she was getting at.

'You and Mack. Are you happy with him again now? I know it unnerved you with what happened to Joe.'

'I think so. I knew I was falling for him, and it felt so right, but so scary.'

'Oh, Mum, that's brilliant.'

Eve smiled. 'I realised over this past week that I need to give me and him a chance.'

Grace's smile morphed into a yawn. 'I think I need to find someone for myself in case I get left behind,' she said.

Eve laughed, glad she had her daughter's approval.

## CHAPTER THIRTY-THREE

'Oh, for crying out loud!' Eve sighed, eyeing the tomato she'd dropped rolling along the bottom of the sink unit. She was all fingers and thumbs this evening. Glancing up at the clock every few seconds, counting down the minutes until their planning would be revealed. She'd feel much better once everything was out in the open.

'Is Mack coming round?' Rose asked, oblivious to her daughter's mood.

'Yes, he is.' Eve beamed.

'He's doing you the world of good, Eve. It's wonderful to see you so happy.'

Eve's smile was because she was feeling slightly manic, not happy, but she wasn't going to say that. Picking up the rogue tomato, she threw it into the bin and continued to put the salad together.

She stared out of the window. It had been a blustery day, the forecasted rain kept at bay, but the trees were swaying, leaves seeming to be hanging on for dear life.

'Autumn is fast approaching,' she said. 'Time is going so quickly. It'll soon be Christmas.'

'You said the C word! It's way too early for that malarkey.' Rose laughed.

Grace smiled, her apprehension around Cedric's visit making her talk gibberish. She was thankful Cedric had agreed to come to her home, though. That way, it would be up to Rose to decide if she wanted to give out her address to him. And if she didn't, then they could spend a few hours together, Cedric could go back to Newcastle, and she could rest that her mum would be safe.

The doorbell went, and she rushed to answer it. She knew it would be Mack as they were eating as a family first.

'Hey.' Mack kissed her and then held up a bottle of wine. 'I thought this might help to steady your nerves.'

'Thanks.' She took it from him. 'I really don't know why I'm so anxious.'

'It's a big moment, for Rose as well as Cedric.' He pulled her into his arms to kiss her again. 'I think it's quite romantic. It's a bit like you and me. Maybe they were meant to be together.'

'Mum's seventy-nine! Hardly much time left if it was meant to be.'

'I know. Still, perhaps they'll make the most of what they have now, like we're doing.'

Eve smiled, pleased that he wasn't pushing her. They'd had a chat about their relationship, neither of them seeing the need to rush things. Most of the time, they were reminiscing more than planning for the future. Yet, she *could* look forward now with the thought of sharing it with him.

Once Grace arrived, Eve dished out the food, and they shared small talk about their days. Underneath the table, Mack squeezed Eve's thigh, and when she looked up, he was smiling at her. It made her feel slightly better, for all of a few seconds.

The clock went round to seven o'clock far too quickly.

Even though she was expecting it, Eve jumped when the doorbell went.

'That'll be Fiona.' Eve got up. 'She said she was calling in. She has a few magazines for me.'

'Ask her in for a glass of wine,' Rose shouted after her. 'It would be nice to see her.'

Eve snorted to herself. A quick glance in the hall mirror showed she was respectable, no food between her teeth and nothing down her top. With a deep breath, she opened the door.

Cedric Brownslow stood before her, dressed in a navy three-piece suit with a paisley tie. He wore a grey Crombie hat and was carrying an enormous bouquet of flowers and a Somerley Stores carrier bag.

'Eve?' he greeted, smiling shyly.

'Yes, yes, come in, Cedric. Did you find us okay?'

'I had a taxi drop me off. In some ways, Somerley is just as I remember, but in others, I can't recall a thing. I'm staying at the B and B, on the high street. It was lovely to see it again. Like a trip along memory lane. Half the places I remember, half of them are new. Time never stands still.'

'Indeed. It's still as sleepy as ever.'

'You have a lovely house.' Cedric stepped inside. 'Have you lived here long?'

'Nearly thirty years. I never felt the need to move.'

He handed her the carrier bag. 'These are for you, chocolates and a bottle of wine. The flowers are for Rose, of course.'

'Thank you, you shouldn't have.' Eve popped them all on the hall table. 'For me, I mean, not Rose.'

Eve took his coat and hat afterwards, and then they stood in silence for a few seconds. Cedric ran a hand over his bald head and glanced around.

'Are you ready to go through?' she asked him.

Cedric nodded fervently. 'I've waited a long time for this.'

Eve reached for his arm, giving it a squeeze. She had a good feeling about this now she'd met Cedric in person.

She opened the kitchen door. Rose was talking to Mack and Grace, who immediately looked her way.

'Mum, there's someone here to see you.' There was a slight tremor in Eve's voice.

'I thought you said it would be Fiona for you.' Rose turned in her chair.

Eve stepped aside to allow Cedric to be visible to her.

'Hello, Rose.' Cedric smiled shyly.

Rose's face was a picture when she spotted him. She stood up quickly, arms wide, and then hugged him, no words coming from her.

Eve's eyes burned with tears she didn't want to fall. The love Rose had for Cedric was said so much with that one gesture. How had her mother missed a life with someone who made her feel that way? The chance to be with someone who would have given her love back and, more to the point, respected her as a woman?

Mack and Grace were silent, too. Finally, Rose spoke. But it wasn't to Cedric. It was to Eve and Grace.

'How?' she asked.

'I'm afraid we've been a bit crafty. Cedric realised he hadn't included any contact details in his letter to you, so he emailed Grace with his address,' Eve explained. 'We thought it best if you met with family around you first.'

'We had to vet him, Gran,' Grace added. 'To make sure he was who he says he is.' It earned her a swift nudge in the ribs from her mum.

'Oh, he's definitely my Cedric.' Rose put a hand to his face.

Mack began to clear away the plates. 'Why don't you all

go through to the living room and leave me to clear up in here?'

'I'll help. It won't take a moment.' Eve picked up the empty salad bowl.

'I know, but I can do it.'

'Actually, could I see Cedric alone for a moment?' Rose questioned. 'I just want to see if he's real.'

'Oh, I'm real, all right.' Cedric laughed.

As they left the room together, Grace leaned back in her chair. 'That was a turn up for the books. I've never seen Gran looking so happy.'

Eve nodded, her bottom lip trembling again.

Mack nudged her. 'Don't get all maudlin on us now,' he teased. 'Let's get these dishes put in the washer and top up the wine.'

'Oh, I have much better than that.' Eve opened the fridge and pulled out a bottle of champagne. 'This calls for a celebration!'

## CHAPTER THIRTY-FOUR

Grace had felt sneaky keeping her thoughts about Della from Flora. But when she saw Della going into the ladies', on the spur of the moment she followed her. A couple of minutes later, Grace orchestrated it so that she came out of her cubicle at the same time Della opened the door to hers.

'Can I talk to you about something?' she asked, washing her hands in the sink beside her. 'It's a bit delicate, but I don't know who else I can trust.'

'Of course.' Della was all ears. 'What's the matter?'

Knowing she had piqued Della's curiosity, Grace continued. 'I've had a couple of nasty pen letters and I'm wondering whether I should report them to Tom or ignore them.'

Della wouldn't look Grace in the eye.

'What do you think I should do?' she persisted.

'I'd ignore them,' Della replied.

'I shouldn't be worried about them?'

'No. It's just some prankster. I know it isn't very nice, but I've had worse.'

'Have you?'

'Lots of times – mostly by email, though. Haven't you?'

'Not really.' It was Grace's time to fib. 'The thing is, it must be someone from inside the office. There's no stamp on the envelope.'

'Someone could have hand-delivered them, posting them through our letter box.'

'They didn't. Flora and I have been checking the camera footage.' Technically speaking, they had seen a bit of it.

Della, intent on checking out her makeup, pouted her lips at herself in the mirror. An uncomfortable silence fell between them, and Grace hoped no one came into the room until this was over.

She stared at Della now, watching for signs she knew more. By the heat rising up from her chest, Grace could tell something was troubling her, but how would she broach the subject without getting angry? If she was right, she wanted to rip into Della, explain the hurt and stress she'd caused her.

And yet, even though she wasn't sure what it was all about, something was telling her not to. She wanted to hear her what she had to say first.

When Della moved towards the exit, Grace blocked her way.

'I think I have to tell Tom about them,' she said. 'What happens if someone from here wants to get back at me for something I don't know I've done? I need to trust the people I work with. It doesn't seem right not to say anything.'

'Anyone could have put them in your in-tray for a joke.'

'A joke? It's not even funny.' Grace folded her arms. 'Okay, then I'll ask all the staff before I say anything to Tom.'

'No!' Della cried, her eyes widening. 'Can't you just forget them, until you get another one perhaps?'

'Thing is, Della, they've gone missing.' Grace shrugged. 'One minute they were in my drawer, and now I can't find them.'

'Maybe whoever sent them felt guilty and got rid of them?'

'Hmm. It was you, wasn't it?'

'Of course it wasn't.' Della's cheeks burned.

'I know it was. While you were on holiday, I was looking over your handwriting.' Another white lie, Grace was on a roll. 'I don't know why I didn't do it sooner. I suppose with most admin done online these days, I don't see your lettering often. But there's no mistaking the way you write letters D and T.'

Della's shoulders flopped. 'I'm sorry.'

'So it was you?' Grace cried. 'But why?'

'I don't know.' Della burst into tears. 'Please don't say anything to Tom. I'm in enough trouble as it is for being late all the time, and if I tell him the reason why, he'll probably fire me anyway. I'm in such a mess. I can't concentrate from one minute to the next.'

All Grace's anger disappeared at the pain in Della's outburst. She manoeuvred Della towards the stool in the corner and fetched some toilet roll for her to wipe her eyes.

'My mum has dementia, and there's only me at home to help with her care,' Della said eventually. 'That's why I'm often late. Either I haven't been able to leave her on time as she's in a bit of a state, or I've overslept because she's kept me away during the night. I don't know whether I'm coming or going half the time, and it's getting worse.' She wiped at her nose. 'That's why I went away for a week. My brother had her staying at his house, and it was enough for him to realise how much I have to cope with every day.'

Grace didn't know what to say. She'd known something was wrong, but she hadn't expected that. 'Why didn't you tell Tom about your mum?'

'Because the job is temporary, and I assumed he'd work

out that it was happening way before I arrived here. I lied to him.'

'It wouldn't have made a difference if you were honest.' Grace paused. Despite Della being upset, she still wanted to know more. 'It doesn't explain why you sent those letters to me, though.'

'I was jealous. You're really well liked here, and I was getting it in the neck from Tom all the time for being late, and I just wanted to sabotage your project. It was a stupid thing to do.'

'Yes, it was.' Seeing Della's bottom lip trembling, Grace relented. 'It's a good job I haven't told anyone what's been happening, even though I still don't understand what you'd get out of it.'

'I really am sorry.' Della wiped at her eyes. 'I didn't want to send anymore after two, and I thought because you hadn't said anything that I could get them out from your desk and forget it ever happened.'

'So you did go into my desk.'

'Yes, that was me.' Della sniffed. 'What are you going to do about it?'

The million-dollar question. Really, Della needed to be disciplined for what she'd done, but Grace couldn't see any purpose in getting her into trouble for it.

What would her mum do? She knew the answer to that straightaway. So she decided to be grown up about the issue.

'There's no harm done,' she said, 'apart from me being stressed about it, and blaming my ex a couple of times.'

'Oh God. Sorry!'

'Don't worry about that.' She wafted away the comment. All of a sudden, she felt the need to protect Della. She didn't want anything else to add to her worries, even if it had been a childish thing to do. And who knows if this episode would tip her over the edge.

Grace knew she was being a pushover but decided to show a little leniency.

'If you promise not to do anything like it again, I'll forget it happened,' she said.

'You'd do that for me?'

'Well, I would for two white chocolate and raspberry cupcakes.'

Grace was taken by surprise as Della gave her a hug. 'Thank you. I really am sorry.'

Grace hugged her back. 'I'll leave you in here to tidy yourself up.'

Della smiled through more tears.

Once back at her desk, Grace tried to get her head around what had happened and how to keep it away from Flora. If there were no more letters, it would blow over anyway.

# CHAPTER THIRTY-FIVE

Once Rose had got over the initial shock of seeing Cedric, she was feeling excited about seeing him again today. Yesterday at Eve's home had been overwhelming, emotional, and yet the meeting had been full of joy. She and Cedric hadn't managed a lot of time to talk, so he was coming round that morning.

She must have tried on every outfit that she owned, throwing them all on the bed with dismay. Then she'd sat down next to the pile of clothes and realised that Cedric was coming to see her, not what she was wearing.

They had both obviously changed so much since their early twenties but, even so, she could remember everything about him as if it were yesterday. She wished she'd been with him as he'd grown into his wrinkles, seen the age spots appearing, the tiny bit of extra weight around his middle, and his hair loss.

She wondered if he remembered her, before her hair had greyed and her eyesight had diminished. She'd definitely put a little more weight around her middle. But then, it was almost sixty years since they'd seen each other.

When he'd appeared in Eve's kitchen, she'd been taken straight back to the last time she'd seen him. They had been in the work's canteen; she was sitting with Iris and a group of women while they ate their lunch. Harry had gone to the shops to fetch some cigarettes.

Cedric had been across the way, on a table with his friends. He'd waved at her, and she'd smiled and dropped her eyes. When she'd looked at him again, he'd beckoned her over and given her a note. Her eyes had widened in excitement when she'd read it. He was asking her to meet him at the back of the building. He wanted to talk to her.

She hadn't told Iris where she was going. She knew she wouldn't be long because their break was over in ten minutes. Still, she wished there had been time to freshen up. She barely had any lipstick left to brighten her face.

Her heart had been in her mouth when she'd opened the back door and saw him waiting for her in the car park. He'd reached for her hand and pulled her out of sight.

'I can't stop thinking about you,' he'd said, gazing into her eyes.

Rose remembered her stomach fizzing, something that hadn't happened when Harry was so near to her.

'You're in my every thought,' he'd gone on. 'I can tell that you like me, too, but I know you're seeing Harry and I—'

'It's nothing serious!' she'd almost shouted before lowering her voice.

Cedric tilted her chin up and moved closer still. 'Harry seems to think so.'

'We've only seen each other a few times. He's...' Rose had trailed off, not daring to air her thoughts.

'Do you like me, Rose? As much as I like you?'

'I... I think so.'

'Good, because I need to do this.' He'd leaned in and kissed her.

At first, Rose had been hesitant, yet suddenly she couldn't help but draw Cedric closer to her. And from that moment on, she had wanted to be with him.

She'd told Cedric she would finish things with Harry that weekend, and then they would have to keep their relationship secret for a while so as not to make it awkward at work.

That was the last time she'd seen him. By Monday morning he was gone, and he'd taken her heart with him.

And then she'd stayed with Harry.

Rose hadn't long been married when things had changed for the worse. Before they were wed, she and Harry had a respectable relationship. He'd treated her well, bought her gifts, and when he'd proposed after a few months, she'd happily accepted.

Their wedding had been a small one, in a registry office. Although Rose would have preferred to be married in a church, Harry insisted they could put the money to better use decorating a house he had his eye on. To keep numbers down, they'd chosen three friends and their partners each, and only close relatives.

'I'm not feeding anyone I haven't seen in years,' Harry had moaned. 'My mother will have to tell the uncles, aunts, and cousins that they don't have invites.'

Rose hadn't minded so much at the time, caught up in the wedding fever. But Iris had seen things differently. The night before she was due to be married, her friend had pulled her to one side.

'Are you sure you're doing the right thing?' she'd asked her.

'Of course,' Rose had replied.

'You haven't been together long.'

'I know, but we love each other. Isn't that obvious?'

Iris had gone to speak but seemed to think better of it. But Rose had wanted to know.

'What's wrong? Don't you like Harry?'

'He's a bit... controlling.'

Rose had laughed. 'I admit he's protective, but it's nice to have someone who cares so much.'

'I suppose,' Iris had relented. 'As long as you're happy, that's the main thing.'

In that instant, Rose had assumed Iris was jealous. She'd just ended a relationship that had gone on for six months. With Rose getting hitched to Harry, they wouldn't have a lot of time together, like they used to.

It wasn't until later years that Rose realised just how much Iris had seen in Harry during those few months of courtship. She wished she had taken more notice.

So it would be good to find out why Cedric had left Somerley so suddenly and see if the rumours that had circulated about him had been true. Rose had never believed them.

And yet, here she was, nervous yet excited about seeing him again. He was coming to her home. She had so much to tell him, but where to begin?

Cedric arrived on the dot of midday. Rose was waiting in the kitchen so rushed to the door to let him in.

He had that wonderful smile, the one he'd worn last night. Rose's heart beat so loud she was sure he would hear it. They stood like statues for a moment until Cedric spoke.

'Hello again, Rose,' he said.

'Cedric.' Rose ushered him into the living room. 'I still can't get over your accent. You're all why aye, man.'

'Living in Newcastle for the best part of your life will do that to you. What a lovely place you have.' He glanced around, taking it all in. 'Have you lived here long?'

'Three years, since... since Harry died.'

Even the mention of his name didn't bring down the mood. They couldn't take their eyes off each other and in two steps were in each other's arms. It felt so good to be alone with him. To feel his warmth surrounding her, his hand resting on her back, his heart beating in her ear.

She made tea, and they chatted as they sat on the settee next to each other.

'I'm so glad Grace managed to track you down,' she said. 'Why didn't you put in your contact address?'

'I'd sealed the envelope and posted it before I realised I hadn't.' Cedric grimaced. 'In fact, it took me a few days to recall.'

She laughed. 'Is Somerley how you remember it?'

'I haven't seen much of it yet. I was hoping you might show me around. I'm here for a few days before I leave.'

Rose didn't want to think about that, but she did want to know one thing. 'Why didn't you ever come back to Somerley?'

'Back then, I was embarrassed for giving up so easily. And then I met Betty. I had a wonderful life with her. But when I saw you on the TV, a rush of feelings came over me, and I knew I had to try and see you, whether you were still with Harry or not.'

They chatted about their lives in general, and then Cedric placed a hand over Rose's.

'I need to tell you the reason why I left,' he said. 'It wasn't because I didn't want to be with you. Someone saw us together that lunch time, and they told Harry.'

# CHAPTER THIRTY-SIX

Rose didn't know what to say. She dreaded what was coming next.

'Harry followed me home that evening,' Cedric continued. 'He told me to leave you alone, that you were his. Well, I wasn't having that, so I told him to bugger off. We got into a fight, stupid really. But he came at me, so I had to defend myself. When I'd got the better of him, and we'd calmed down enough to speak, he told me you were getting married because you were pregnant.'

'None of that was true,' Rose cried.

'I wasn't sure I believed him anyway. I could sense he would do anything to keep you. I had to admire him for that.' Cedric smiled. 'I was going to speak to you about it on Monday. But then, over the weekend, I was set upon by several men from the factory. They told me to sling my hook and never come back. I was scared, Rose. They nearly killed me. The reason I didn't come to work on Monday to see you was because they put me in hospital.'

Rose's hand flew to her mouth. She had known none of this.

'Harry had clout with the people around him. I just thought, for your sake, I'd be better leaving. He would have only made things worse, for you as much as me. I'm afraid I let the bully win. I'm not proud of myself for giving in to him, but I made the decision it was better all round if I left.

'When I got back to my flat, it had been trashed. Harry must have found out where I was living. I didn't have much, but most of it was ruined. So I grabbed what I could and went to stay with my aunt in Newcastle. I got a job and tried to forget you. It was hard at times. I wanted to write a letter to you, but I didn't know your address. In the end, time was the only healer I had. I met Betty a year later, and we were married for forty-six years before she died.'

'I wish I had known how deceitful Harry had been,' Rose told him. 'I would have rushed after you. It broke my heart when you left. But Harry told me you'd been stealing from the factory shop and had been sacked.'

'That's not true either.' Cedric gave a faint smile.

'He said you'd left in disgrace. He could always be persuasive. I had no reason not to believe him because I couldn't speak to you to find out the truth. So, like you, I tried to get on with my life without you. Harry was kind to me then, giving me lots of attention. We married eventually, but it wasn't a happy marriage.' Rose's eyes brimmed with tears. 'I swear to you, Cedric, that I wasn't pregnant, and I never forgot you.'

'Nor I you.' Cedric covered her hand with both of his.

Rose looked into his eyes. How could he be here, sitting so close to her? She'd thought she'd never see him again.

Then she took a deep breath and told him what life with Harry had been really like.

'He was a bully to me, and Eve, all his life. He controlled me, my finances, and saw to it that I was totally under his thumb. He used to laugh at me all the time, make me the butt of his jokes so everyone else would laugh, too. He made me so nervous, clumsy, because he would pick fault with everything I did. He wouldn't tell me things and then say that I'd forgotten to do something when I didn't even know he wanted me to do it. He put me down in front of people, and in the house he was even worse.'

'Oh, love. Why did you stay with him?'

'I couldn't find a way out, if I'm honest, and I did love him in my own way. For the first few years anyway. I had a time of staying pregnant when we eventually tried for a baby, so when Eve came along and was so precious, I thought it was best that we stayed as a family. It's the biggest regret of my life.'

'He wasn't... violent with you, was he?'

Rose paused. How much should she tell him?

About the night when Eve had come home from the pictures to find them arguing and him throwing things at her in the kitchen.

About the time when they were on holiday and he'd gone missing overnight, returning first thing in the morning after she'd worried about him for hours.

About the first affair, or the second.

About the month she'd managed to leave with Eve when she was seven, eventually being persuaded to come back and give it another go. He'd slapped her as soon as they got home, threatening all sorts if she ever attempted to leave again.

'Every now and then he would lose his temper completely and I'd come off worse,' she said eventually. 'But it was more controlling behaviour than anything. And he could be really nice every now and then. I think he loved me in his own stupid way, and I blame his parents because his mother and father were the same.

'I tried to change him into something better, but he didn't like any suggestions. In the end, it was easier to let him have his way. He made me feel worthless. A failure for staying with him, and for being a terrible wife.'

'If you were married to me, Rose, I would have told you every day how beautiful you are. I would have said I loved you before we went to bed every night. I would have treated you with the respect and dignity that you deserved.'

'And I would have loved you for it.' She smiled. 'I can't believe how stupid I was now. But it was easier to put up with him. He wasn't terrible all the time. He could be charming, and loving, and funny. And you should see how he doted on Grace. She doesn't know any of this, by the way, and I'd like it to stay between us.'

'Of course.' Cedric took her hand in his own. 'For what it's worth, I think you were brave to go through what you did.'

'I don't think I was—'

'It wasn't as easy in our day to up sticks and leave, even if you had somewhere to go. So for you to put Eve first shows how much you would sacrifice to keep your daughter safe and happy.'

'I'm not sure she wasn't scarred from it. She lived through it all, that undercurrent of never being able to do as she pleased, not getting anything right.'

'I suppose you'll never know how much that has affected her, I admit. But she seems a wonderful, warm person from what I've seen of her so far. You must have been doing something right.'

Rose smiled.

Cedric pulled out a bundle of envelopes wrapped in an elastic band and gave them to her.

'I wrote to you every year, even though I knew I'd be in terrible trouble if Betty found them. She told me before she died that she had.'

'No!' Rose squeaked.

'Yes, but she wasn't angry. That was my Betty for you. She said I should track you down, but I never found the courage. So they were my way of keeping in touch with you, even though it was one-sided. I never forgot you, Rose Machin.'

There were so many, all unopened. Rose would have to be alone when she read them for fear of shedding too many tears.

Some fell now, anyway, when she looked up at Cedric. Saw the love in his eyes. She had never seen that in Harry's.

Rose cried then, for the life she could have had.

# CHAPTER THIRTY-SEVEN

Despite everyone being happy that Rose had been reunited with Cedric, Grace wasn't too enamoured. At work, when she'd explained the situation, Tom thought it would be a good idea to run an article on the couple's reunion, with their permission, in next week's paper. After chatting to her gran to see that she and Cedric were fine about it, Grace had been tasked with writing the piece.

It wasn't something she really wanted to do. Grace assumed Tom thought she would enjoy it because it was her family, but there was something niggling her about the whole situation. It all seemed so... easy.

Putting on her investigative hat, she wrote down a list of questions she needed to find answers for and then arranged to see her gran on Saturday morning.

After a restless Friday night, she went downstairs to find her mum in the kitchen.

'Morning, love.' Eve greeted her with a smile. 'I was just about to get some breakfast. Do you fancy toast with your cereal?'

'Yes, thanks, Mum. I'll make more tea.'

The radio was on low, and they moved around the room in a companionable silence before sitting at the table once everything was ready.

'How are you getting on with the article?' Eve asked, brushing crumbs from her chest onto her plate. 'Can I help with anything you want to know, before you go to see Gran?'

Grace thought for a moment. Should she say what she was worried about, or would it be better talking it through with Gran?

She spat it out regardless.

'Actually, there is something. How long do you think Cedric will hang around before he goes back to Newcastle?'

'What do you mean?' Eve's brow furrowed. 'He's not long arrived.'

'I know, but he didn't come back for years.' Her skin reddened. 'I'm just a little suspicious, that's all, and I don't want to see Gran getting hurt.'

'I think she's old enough to make her own mind up about things. She is nearly eighty.'

'Which is why I don't want him taking advantage of her. For all we know, he might not have a home in Newcastle and want to come and live with Gran so he can fleece her out of all her money.'

'What money?' Eve shook her head. 'She doesn't have a lot.'

'I didn't mean—'

'You don't seriously think that Cedric is out to con Gran?'

'I wouldn't put it past him.'

'Why?'

Grace shrugged like a petulant child.

Eve sat forwards. 'Grace, your gran deserves a bit of happiness.'

'She had a lot, when she was with Granddad.'

Eve huffed. 'How little you know.'

'What do you mean?'

Eve gnawed at her bottom lip. 'Let's just say your granddad wasn't the nicest man to get along with.'

'He seemed fine to me.'

'You didn't know him the way I did, like your gran did.'

It was Grace's turn to sit forwards. 'What's going on?'

'I hate to sully your memory, but things were never happy with your grandparents. Harry wasn't a nice man. He had a violent temper, sometimes your gran got the wrath of him, and I had to—'

'Wait a minute,' Grace interrupted. 'Are you saying Granddad hit Gran?'

'I'm afraid so. And not just the once either.'

Grace closed her eyes momentarily to rid herself of the images flashing in her mind. Her granddad slapping her gran; her gran reeling from its force.

'We never spoke about it, your gran and I, until he died, but we looked out for each other until that moment. I suppose we protected ourselves without saying a word.'

'Did he hit you, too?'

Eve nodded.

Grace almost crumbled. How could this be true?

'He'd take his anger out on me if Gran wasn't around,' Eve went on. 'It was usually after he'd been to the pub and, whenever he did, Gran would have a go at him. He'd be sorry for it afterwards. But always, the next day, she would have bruising on her face, or be holding her stomach with the pain of what he'd done to her. He was a brute.'

'So why did she marry him?'

'He charmed her, made out she was his world. And afterwards, he changed. She told me she became a shell of her original self. He told her what to wear, that she couldn't go out with her friends while he was out all the time. He made her do everything over and over until she got things to his satisfaction, which was usually never. He took her life from her.'

Even though this was her granddad, the man she had looked up to all her life, they were discussing, Grace was finding it hard not to be disgusted.

'There's no way I'd stay with someone like that. Why didn't she leave him?'

'Firstly because he told her over and over that she couldn't cope without him, that no one else would want her. He never gave her any money, so she was trapped. Once I came along, she was more mindful of providing a roof over our heads to protect me.

'Secondly, back in the sixties, it wasn't the done thing to divorce. So she stuck with him. And I know that because, when he died, she told me that she regretted every minute of it. She said she was a coward not to leave, but I think she was really brave for what she put up with. She protected me as best she could.'

Grace pulled a face. 'Why didn't *she* tell me?'

'Because you idolised your granddad and she didn't want to ruin your memories of him!'

'Oh.'

'So when Cedric got in touch, it seemed like fate. She was so happy to see him.'

Grace hung her head in shame. Here she was, thinking all sorts of things about Cedric, when it appeared he was a better man than her granddad.

'I feel stupid.'

'I'm sorry, love. I didn't want to tell you, but I think maybe now is the right time it was out in the open. Please go easy on them. Gran deserves happiness after all this time, and I'm sure she'll be upset if you were going to talk to her about what we've discussed, because she won't want to hurt you. But, well, none of us is getting any younger, so we have to take the opportunity to be happy when we can. Just like I am with Mack.'

She reached across the table, covering Grace's hand with her own.

'It doesn't mean I love your dad any less. It means that I can love someone else differently from now on. Mack reminds me of your dad in so many ways, and yet in others he comes across as his own man. He's wounded by his past, too, and one day he might tell you about that. We all are, to a certain extent, especially when you've lived as many years of life as we have.'

'You oldies, you're all drama.' Grace rolled her eyes in jest.

## CHAPTER THIRTY-EIGHT

It was ten o'clock when Grace arrived at Somerley Heights. Rose came bustling to the door and gave her a hug.

'I've been talking to Mum earlier,' Grace said. 'About Cedric.'

'Ah. I was going to make a cup of tea, but that can wait. Come through to the front room.'

Grace sat next to Rose on the settee, the sound of hedge cutters in the background coming through the open window.

'I wasn't really happy about Cedric coming to see you,' she admitted. 'I thought he was trying to muscle in on Granddad's memories and I didn't like it, so instead I told Mum I didn't trust him and that he might be out to con you. I didn't want him to meet you.'

Rose roared with laughter. 'Cedric hasn't got a bad bone in his body.'

Grace blushed at her ridiculous notion. 'Mum has been telling me what Granddad put you through when you were younger. Why did you keep it from me?'

'Oh, it was different back in my day. We just put up and shut up. Not like women of today, who can have a voice and get out of a situation if they can find the courage. Because you see, I was a coward.'

'I don't believe that for a second.'

Rose took a deep breath. 'It might help if I tell you why Cedric left to go to Newcastle and why he never came back.'

Grace listened to what her gran had to say, all the time getting angrier. How could her granddad have done that to Cedric, and then be so coercive with her gran? And how had she not seen any of it?

Or had she? Had she ignored what was right under her nose, so as not to accept the truth?

As she'd driven over in the car, she'd recalled her granddad always snapping at her gran. Rose could never do anything right; he'd be moaning about her being clumsy, the food being too hot or too cold. His clothes had to be ironed just so, and the home was always spick and span. More like a show house than a home.

And all the time, Grace had thought he was a wonderful man. Like he was laughing *with* her gran, and not at her, when she could see now that it had been the other way round.

She couldn't really blame herself as she'd been young and impressionable, and her gran had hidden her pain well. So when any doubt popped up, she could easily think it was all in her mind, that it was how her gran and granddad were.

Now, shame washed over her for not seeing him for what he was.

And how could she think that Cedric was out to trick her, too? Her gran wasn't a foolish woman who he could fleece. Her gran was a strong, independent woman. She'd always taught Grace right from wrong, admonished her when she'd needed it, praised her when she had done something well. To think that she'd been hiding all her suffering was unthinkable.

'When I lost your granddad,' Rose went on, 'I was so relieved, and I felt guilty for that. So I wrote him a letter. I told him how terrible he had treated me over the years. Things I should have said while he was alive, but you know him, he never let me get a word in edgewise.' She smiled, almost shyly. 'Anyway, I was going to shove it in the pocket of his suit when I buried him.'

'Gran, you didn't,' Grace cried.

'Of course I didn't. Sometimes it's easier to write a letter than to say the words out loud to someone. Just the act of writing it made me let it go. I felt as if I'd told him. So I ripped it up into tiny little pieces and threw it away. That's why I thought of the letter project for you, but with a happy theme. It was more like my redemption for thinking horrid thoughts.'

'You don't have a nasty bone in your body either, Gran.' Grace gave her a hug, squeezing her tightly.

Rose kissed her cheek. 'I wish I had because I'd have stuck up for myself all those years ago and left. When I got married, there was no such thing as women's refuges or places of safety. In fact, in the seventies it was looked upon as a good thing to hit your wife. To keep her in line.' Rose huffed. 'That's not from me, by the way. I read an article about it online, so I know it didn't just happen to me. Pretty shocking, really.'

'That's disgusting.' Grace shook her head. 'I'm glad in this day and age that women and men in bad relationships have somewhere to go. It can't always be easy for them, especially if children are involved.' Her brain began to tick over. 'I'm going to pitch a project on this. I think it would be another topic to mix with the old and the new. How the younger generation won't put up with it as much, ultimately because there is help out there. Places to go, people to turn to. But also regarding the toxicity of today's world, the danger of online dating and social media gaslighting.'

Rose cupped Grace's face and smiled. 'Grace, you were born to tell stories. I am so proud of you.'

Driving home, Grace thought back over their conversation. Looking back on things, she could see a lot of her gran and granddad's relationship in the four years she'd spent with Liam. He'd wanted to control Grace, but she'd stood her ground, which was why they'd split up.

She might have had fuzzy feelings about him many moons ago but, towards the end, she couldn't remember the last time her face had lit up when he'd smiled at her. He'd become a habit rather than her future, yet she hadn't wanted to do anything about it until he'd forced her hand.

Her thoughts turned to Tyler then. Because she didn't just get a stomach flip when he smiled at her. She got a whole emotional roller coaster of feelings that she never wanted to stop.

All gran wanted was a second chance, to be happy with Cedric. It was the same for her mum and Mack. Maybe Grace needed a second chance of her own.

Perhaps with someone like Tyler?

## CHAPTER THIRTY-NINE

Della was having a well-earned break. After bottoming the house and settling her mum for a nap, she needed a caffeine pick-me-up and a sugary treat. As she bit into a doughnut, she thought that if she had time before work on Monday morning, she would call into The Coffee Stop and get cakes for everyone. She particularly wanted to get Grace her favourite, maybe two again.

Even now, she cringed at the thought of what she'd done. More to the point, Grace had been so nice about it. Della wasn't sure she would have been that charitable. Those notes had been mean, meant to hurt Grace even though she hadn't really got to know her by then.

Grace had welcomed her from the moment they'd started working together. It worried Della that the job was temporary, and she'd been hoping to get a permanent position in the meantime. Not especially at *Somerley News* but at anywhere in the town. Nothing suitable had come up yet, though, so she was thankful she still had a job there. Stupid, stupid Della.

A car pulled up outside, catching her eye. She sat up a little, allowing her to see through the window. It was her brother, and he was on his own. He didn't usually call on a Saturday afternoon. He'd be off playing golf, or watching the boys playing football, perhaps getting dragged around the shops with Jenny if he was unlucky.

Even though he had a key, she went to let Chris in.

'I didn't expect to see you, today,' she said as he stepped inside.

'I wanted to talk to you about something. Is Mum downstairs? We can go out in the garden if so.'

'She's having a nap, upstairs. What's wrong?'

Della followed him into the living room.

Chris sat down, his face a mask of worry. 'What I'm about to say won't be easy to listen to. But, until you went away, Jenny and I had no idea what you had to put up with each day with Mum.'

'It's hardly putting up with her, Chris,' Della bristled, sitting across from him on the settee. 'She's our mum.'

'I know, but until we had to step in to take care of her, I hadn't realised how much pressure it put on you. We didn't have a spare minute, constantly being on watch. It was like having a toddler at times, tantrums, tears, running away.'

'She ran away?' Della sat upright. 'You never told me that.'

'She only got three houses down one morning, but it made me realise how dangerous it is for her to be alone.'

'I have to go out to work, and we have assistance with basic needs twice a day. If you and Jenny could help out more, then I'd be able to cope better.'

'That's why you went away, isn't it? Not for the break, but to show us how it is for you.'

'No, not at all.' She paused. 'I did need a break from it, though.'

'I get it, it's a lot for you to do by yourself.'

'If you could have her to stay every other weekend, or

maybe a couple of nights during the week, to give me a break, that would be great. And then—'

'Jenny and I think she should go into residential care.'

A sickly feeling whooshed around Della's stomach as his words sank in. 'You want to put Mum in a home? After all she's done for us?'

'She needs round-the-clock care, and we can't give that to her.'

'How would you know?' Della clenched her hands.

'A week was hard enough for us.'

'Oh, poor you. Cramp your style, did she?'

'There's no need to be snappy, Del.' Chris ran a hand through his hair. 'I'm not comfortable about it, but she's far worse than I imagined because you cover it up so well.'

'I've done my best, and all of a sudden it isn't enough?'

'Without you, she wouldn't have been able to stay at home for this long. But you've seen the letter from the consultant. She's deteriorating.'

'We can get in extra help.' A tear dripped down Della's cheek, and she wiped it away quickly.

'You're not being fair to Mum either. We're trying to ease your burden.'

'Our mother is not a burden!'

They sat in silence. Della was transported to a time when they were younger, giving each other the silent treatment after a fight until one of them relented. Sometimes it would go on for days, and their parents would have to intervene. It was a battle of wills. It seemed it was happening again, but there was no one there to stop it this time.

'Just think about it,' Chris said at last. 'That's all we're asking.'

'I've thought of nothing else for the past few months!' She stood up. 'The answer is no. I will not give up on Mum, not like you.'

'She needs to be somewhere they can cope with her condition rather than with us fumbling about in the dark.' He pulled a business card from his pocket and handed it to her. 'There's a spare room here at the moment. We think she should have it.'

'Somerley Heights.' Della shook her head. 'Have you been to view it before asking me?'

'No, but I have made an appointment for us both to go tomorrow morning. Jenny will sit with Mum.' Chris stood up now, reaching out to her. 'Please, Della.'

She stepped back from him. 'She stays here, with me.'

'You can't do this on your own, and it's going to get much worse.'

'I think you should go before I say something I regret.'

He moved towards the door. But then tears poured down her cheeks at the enormity of what was happening.

'Don't go, Chris,' she said quietly.

He came towards her, and she fell into his arms. It was a few minutes before she was able to compose herself enough to talk to him.

"You're right. I do need help.' She grabbed a tissue from a box on the coffee table and blew her nose before continuing. 'I can barely cope with Mum now, and I do worry what she'll be like in the future.'

'We knew you would have struggled on. But you have to think of yourself, too.'

'I know.' It had been a shock to see Chris turning up, but now she was warming to the idea of looking into things. Maybe it wouldn't hurt to see one of the rooms.

'Did you mean what you said about showing me around?' she queried.

'Absolutely.'

Della nodded. 'Go on then, but I'm making no promises.'

# C IS FOR CEDRIC

*Dear Grace,*

*I wanted to write you a letter, but obviously I don't want you to add it to your project.*

*One of the best days of my life was when I met Cedric. Do you believe in love at first sight? Because that's what happened. And that's what your granddad saw.*

*I fell in love with Cedric from the very first time I saw him in the work's canteen. I'd been seeing Harry for about a month. I wasn't sure if it would be serious or not, but he was good fun. Yet I didn't get that fuzzy feeling, you know? The one that makes your stomach flip with the sight of a smile. A cock of the head. A hand engulfing your own. A door held open.*

*I never had that with your granddad. I thought he was wonderful, and I did love him, but he wasn't a joy to be around. He was quite a harsh man. I won't say any more than that now.*

*So another marvellous moment in my life was seeing Cedric again when he walked into your mum's kitchen. I can still remember wondering how he was there, after all that time, not able to believe my eyes. Thank you for bringing him back to me.*

*I'm sorry if it sullies the memory of your granddad. I never meant for that to happen, and there are things that me, nor your mum, will ever tell you. The thing is, Grace, we don't need to. You adored Harry because he was loving and kind to you, and that's all that mattered.*

*I hope you'll indulge me in a little friendship with Cedric. We have a lot of time to catch up on. I know I'm going to enjoy that.*

*All my love,*
*Gran*

# CHAPTER FORTY

Eve held open the door to The Coffee Stop, glancing around to see if there were any empty tables. Rose walked through it just as she spotted one at the back of the room.

'Grab those seats, Mum.' She pointed to it. 'I'll join the queue. The usual coffee and cake?'

'I would love that.'

'Hi, Eve.' Kate, the proprietor, smiled. 'Are you alone or with company?'

'It's me and Mum today.'

'Your usual order?'

'Yes, please.'

'I hear Grace is doing wonderful things regarding the letter project. I sent one of my own in. It was printed in the newspaper.' She threw a thumb over her shoulder.

Eve saw the cutting taped on the wall and smiled. 'It was a lovely letter, Kate. We all miss Lily and Bernard, but you and Chloe did them proud.'

They chatted more as their order was prepared and, once it was ready, Eve took the tray over to join her mum.

'Carrot cake and cappuccino for madam.' Eve placed them on the table. 'And tea and a coffee and walnut slice for me.'

'I bet Grace will be relieved when the project is finished,' Rose said, stirring sugar into her drink. 'It's all anyone is talking about, who is going to win first prize.'

Grace had managed to bag a three-night stay for a family in one of the new lodges at Sapphire Lake in return for a few special features she was going to write. Eve recalled her excitement when she'd told her. Grace had been ecstatic.

'She's done a great job so far.' Eve took the tray back to the counter and then returned. 'When she mentioned that you and I would have to write letters for her, too, I thought it would be easy to come up with the best day in my life.' She smiled fondly. 'Surely it had to be when I met Clark, or when I gave birth to Grace. But honestly? I think the best day in my life was when you were set free from the control of my father.'

Rose was about to eat a mouthful of cake but put down her fork.

'To be fair, he never was a dad, was he?' Eve continued tentatively. 'I lived in constant terror every time I left the house, thinking about the mood he might be in when I got back. If I'd been to school, he was often lurking in the kitchen, ready to grill me about the subjects I'd been taught that day, hoping to trip me up or having a dig at me never getting anywhere as I wasn't clever enough.

'If he'd been out for a drink, and I'd come home from a night out, he'd want to know where I'd been, who I'd spoken to, accuse me of being a flirt, wanting any man who'd look at me. If I was taking an exam, or going for a job interview, he'd put me down before I left the house.' She held in tears as her words hit home a little too much. 'He wanted me to fail. That's why I didn't go to university. I wanted to leave him behind so much, but he made me believe I wasn't strong enough to survive on my own.

'And how could I leave him with you? Without me to cushion some of the blows, he would have been moaning at you all the time. What I saw was enough, the constant put-downs, the laughing at you, the digs that you could get nothing right. I know it sounds strange, and terrible, and disloyal, and abhorrent, and shocking to say that his death was a good thing, but being set free was a happy occasion.'

Eve took a breath after her outburst, for a moment watching the couple next to them as they vacated their table, rather than face her mum. But every word of it was true.

When she composed herself and looked back, Rose was staring at her.

'What's brought all this on?' Rose asked gently.

'Everything that's happened recently, I suppose. I wish I'd told you at the time, but I guess how could I? He really did shape our lives, didn't he? I think I'm only seeing how much now. Because observing you with Cedric, I've never seen you so happy, so vibrant, and the shine in your eyes is wonderful to see. My father never made you feel like that. My father made you into a shell of who you were, and I'm glad to see what must have been the old you returning.'

Tears fell now, and she wiped them away quickly. 'I hope you find comfort in my words. You mean the world to me, Mum, and I have you to thank for me becoming the strong, independent woman I am today.'

'I'm sorry for what happened all those years ago,' Rose said, her voice breaking. 'I wasn't strong enough to leave him, and it ruined your life as much as mine.'

'No, it didn't.' Rose shook her head vehemently. 'It made me insecure, but I was loved by you, and that was enough. I don't want you to ever blame yourself. You did what was best for me, every day.'

'Maybe. Maybe not. Yet I—'

'This isn't about Dad, Mum. It's about you. I want you to make up for all that lost happiness. Have your time with Cedric, go off on cruises, on mini breaks together, whatever makes you light up with joy. I'm grateful for you looking after me for all those years, shielding me from some of the trauma that you went through.' She touched Rose's arm. 'I heard and saw a lot more than you think.'

'Oh, love.'

'Yes, it moulded me into a different person than perhaps I might have been, but I was lucky enough to meet Clark. Because he saw right through Harry, didn't he? Which meant that when he was around, Harry behaved himself. Wasn't that a sight to behold!' Eve was trying to make light of the conversation now. It was becoming too heavy, but she was pleased she'd been able to say the words.

'I miss Clark, Mum, yet I don't miss my father,' she finished. 'But I do love you so very much and am happy that your life is changing for the better. Although you will have to tell Cedric to move back to Somerley if things become more permanent, because I couldn't bear it if you moved to Newcastle.'

Rose was silent for a moment and then burst into laughter. Eve found herself joining in.

## CHAPTER FORTY-ONE

*Dear sixteen-year-old me,*

*I want to tell you not to worry, that everything so far in your life will turn out okay, if not better than you'd hoped.*

*I want you to know that you excel in the written word and end up working at* Somerley News, *which is something you wanted to do since you were a child. I remember you bashing stories out on your little typewriter or walking around with a notepad and pen being an avid reporter or pretending to read the six o'clock news at the kitchen table.*

*I want you to know that you will miss your dad like crazy when he dies suddenly when you're twenty-three. The hurt it will cause you will be immense, grief coming and going like the ebb and flow of the sea. I want you to know that it will never go, it fades, but a song on the radio will remind you of him, a favourite drinking place in summer, a snowball fight in winter. Eventually they'll become treasured memories. But for a long while, they will be too painful to think about. It will be the same for your mum.*

*I want you to know it wasn't your fault that you didn't notice what was going on between Gran and Granddad. You were young, and Gran hid her feelings well. Mum did, too, all to protect you. They don't want you damaged from his behaviour, like they'd been.*

*Their love for you is strong. It will be wonderful to know. And even though your granddad isn't the treasured man you thought he was, he always loved you in his own funny way.*

*I want you to know that I don't blame you for falling in love with Liam and not knowing when to leave when it was all over. For a while, he was the best thing that happened to you, but it all went sour eventually when he became jealous of what you did, of who you were. He lacked ambition and was envious of yours. He really showed his true colours, didn't he? You're far better off without him.*

*And yet you will feel you need to take a chance with someone you've known since you were sixteen. Remember Tyler Walker? The one you snogged one evening behind the working men's club before you found out he was dating Marie Emberson? Well, he became a great friend when you were twenty-one, and yet here we are now, five years on from that, and you sure do have a lot of feelings for him.*

*More importantly, mini-me, I want you to know that you have a wonderful life ahead of you, with friends and family surrounding you, and a career that you love.*

*Everything will be fine, you'll see.*

Grace glanced over the words that she'd written on her laptop. She had come a long way since those awkward teenage years, feeling more confident now than she'd ever been, almost comfortable in her own skin. And if she turned out half as wise as her mum, or her gran, then she had nothing to worry about. Her matriarchal models were the best she could have hoped for.

And, just like her mum and her gran, she had found someone who she'd known for years that she wanted to get to know better.

She reread her letter to herself one more time. And then she deleted it.

Not everything needed to be said aloud.


Grace was rushing around as usual. She'd planned to leave the office early so she could get changed ready for the presentation evening at the community centre, but overseeing things there, to make sure it was all set up perfectly, had left her with barely any time to preen. Della and Flora had been helping to set tables and chairs around the outside of the room. A buffet and themed cupcakes were due to be dropped off half an hour before everyone arrived, and they'd taken it in turns blowing up balloons and hanging banners. All in all, it looked wonderful. It had been a great team effort.

Last week, they'd had a meeting and whittled down the letters to three finalists for the overall prize. Ethan had been shooting short videos of them, as well as getting general feedback from anyone who'd talk to him as he wandered the town.

Now at home, Grace tiptoed across the landing wearing nothing but a towel after a quick shower. She sat down on the bed and ran a comb through her wet hair. Waves of nausea rolled around in her stomach. Why did she feel so nervous? She should be excited, but she wanted everything to be perfect. It was important to finish the project on a positive note.

It was as she reached over for her makeup bag that she spotted the pink envelope propped up beside her mirror. Her name was handwritten on the front.

She opened it, finding a good luck card inside, with a note written from her mum.

. . .

*To the brightest star in the sky,*

*The best day in my life was when you came into the world and were placed in my arms. Honestly, you screamed the place down for the first minute or two, but from that moment on, I knew that our life was complete.*

*Your dad and I doted on you. Spoilt you rotten, our little princess. To be honest, you were an easy baby to look after – I think that was because your dad and I were a team. He wasn't one for leaving everything to me, and because of this, you bonded with him much better than I did with your granddad.*

*You were a smiler, a real chatterbox, too. You were rarely ever quiet – nothing changes there – so there was no doubt in my mind that you'd be a storyteller one day.*

*Congratulations on the success of your first project. It may not have your name against it, but I'm sure it will forever be known as your work. And I'm sure from now on, there will be plenty more things that you lead on.*

*Thank you for making me the proudest of mums, Grace. You are truly an inspiration to anyone of your generation. I am really proud of you.*

*Love Mum x*

A lump formed in Grace's throat, tears spilling down her cheeks. What a lovely thing to do. But that was her mum all over. Warm, kind, thoughtful, and always there for her.

She hoped that would never end, and that Eve would get to spend time with Grace's children one day, passing the best of the Warrington genes on to the next generation. Grace might have lost the men in her life, but the women more than made up for it.

She looked at herself in the mirror, seeing so much of her mum and gran reflected in her. She was a strong, independent woman because of her upbringing. Each day she was thankful for that.

There was a knock at the door, her mum popping her head around it.

'Ah, I see you've opened your card,' she said, almost shyly.

'Thank you.' Grace rushed into her arms. 'For everything you do for me.'

'Works both ways,' Eve replied, hugging her fiercely. 'I meant every word.'

'Even when I'm getting on your nerves being snappy and antsy?'

'Even more so then, grumpy chops.'

They smiled at each other, no words needed. Again.

## CHAPTER FORTY-TWO

Grace pushed open the doors to the community centre, leading into the main room. Music played in the background, and there was a warming sound of chit-chat. Display boards placed around the room contained lots of the letters they'd printed out for show. There were photos, too, taken by Ethan for part of Grace's weekly features, that had been blown up with the writers' details written next to them. Everyone featured had an invite for the evening, and Grace was eager to meet some of the people who had taken the time to write and send in letters.

The first person she spotted was her gran. She was in all her usual finery, the colour scheme this time aqua and baby blue. By her side was Iris, and they were both laughing at something Cedric was saying to them. Grace could almost see the twinkle in Cedric's eyes as he charmed the two women. It brought an instant smile to her face. How wrong she'd been to doubt his intentions.

Cedric caught her eye as she walked towards them. 'Look who's here, Rose,' he said, holding up his hand.

Grace stood next to him. 'Not you again, Cedric,' she

teased. 'Anyone would think you used to live in Somerley many moons ago.'

'Many, many, *many* moons ago,' Rose joined in.

The touch of her hand on Cedric's arm made Grace smile again. But then she spotted someone else snaking his way across the room towards her, and she cried out with pleasure.

'Joe!' Grace rushed into his outstretched arms, enjoying the smell of his cloying aftershave she knew so well.

'Hey, you.' Joe smiled. 'I see the project finished well.'

'It did.' She beamed. 'How are you feeling?'

'Good. Although my lovely wife has been taking care of me, I'm ready to come back to work from next week.'

'As long as you continue to improve.' Fiona rolled her eyes at Grace. 'He's like a bear in a cage at home, though. I'm glad I work full-time!'

'I kept your desk tidy while you weren't there,' Grace said.

Fiona spotted someone, waved, and left them to it.

Even so, Grace leaned in close to Joe and spoke in a conspiratorial whisper. 'There will be a box of doughnuts waiting for you, too. Well, for all of us, but I'll get your favourite as well. Can't have you wasting away.' She patted his stomach playfully.

Joe roared with laughter and gave her another bear hug. 'What am I going to do without listening to your witty rapport every day when I retire?'

'I'll visit, often,' she joked.

She wasn't joking, really.

There were lots of people coming into the room now, hardly a piece of floor to stand on. Grace could see so many residents of Somerley who had turned out for the finale of the project. Staff from most of the shops around the high street and the surrounding streets. Children from the local schools, students from college. The women from the luncheon club and the WI who'd volunteered their services to help some of the groups to work together.

All the staff were there, too. Della was talking to her brother who had come along with her, Riley had joined Ethan, and Ben had brought his girlfriend. Tom's wife, Melissa, was chatting to Fiona and her mum, who had her arm linked through Mack's.

She took a moment to glance around. The buffet table was heaving with everything you could think of. She wanted to pick at it, but she restrained herself until the time was right. At least the balloons and banners had stayed up and intact.

It had all turned out fine, she mused.

'Looking amazing, Grace.' Tyler came up beside her.

'Thanks.' She brushed her hand over her hair, fluttering her eyelids in a comical fashion.

'I meant the room.'

She nudged him in the ribs. 'Of course you did.'

He was about to say something else when the music was lowered, and Tom's voice boomed out of a microphone. He was standing on the makeshift stage, created when there were plays and events going on.

'Ladies and gentlemen. Can I have your attention, please! Thank you all for coming to the presentation evening for The One Letter Project, the idea of our very own Grace Warrington.' Tom raised his glass in a toast, and a cheer went up around the room as everyone did the same.

Grace blushed the colour of an overripe strawberry but grinned back at everyone and lifted her glass high.

Mack whooped, Joe whistled, and laughter spilled over from every corner.

'Like most people, I expect,' Tom said, 'I have a lot of best days in my life, but I want to say something about the day Grace Warrington came to work for *Somerley News*.'

## CHAPTER FORTY-THREE

'It was five years ago that a young, eager, fresh face joined us,' Tom went on. 'First as an admin assistant, and then, as I recognised she was a born storyteller, as a feature assistant. Since then, she's helped to create and work on some exciting projects. Her idea about writing letters was such a simple one yet so effective. It connected the people of Somerley, and beyond due to TV coverage, in a way that I haven't seen since the spirit of the lockdowns.'

A few groans and mumbles went around the room, each person having different recollections of a time they'd most likely want to forget.

'People get lost in their own worlds now, heads stuck in phones or watching Netflix. Lives are busier than ever. There's so much to fit in, as well as social media to scroll endlessly through. All of a sudden we're too busy to cross every t and dot the i's that we forget to check in with the people who we love.

'You see, these might be our best days now, but we all have better ones to come, too. The memories shared this year will be different next year, and the year after. Life is always evolving, showing us good times, and hopefully not too many bad times. We should all embrace the day, as no one is guaranteed tomorrow.'

A hearty round of applause was heard before he continued.

'I think Grace has excelled herself this time, although she won't ever admit it. You see, the thing about Grace is she enjoys nothing more than getting stuck into something she can spread positivity about. And boy, did she find some this time. She made the folk of Somerley smile, as you'll see in a moment from the short film that Ethan, our Digital Production Manager, has created. I think it's only fair that she presents the prizes for the competition. Grace, can you join me on stage, please?'

Grace passed her glass to Tyler, pulled a nervous face at her mum, and then made her way forwards, praying she wouldn't make a fool of herself by tripping up the step. She stood next to Tom, the lights dimmed, and the film came on the screen beside him.

One by one, the three short films about the finalists were played, Grace presented the prize winners with their booty, and just when she was about to step down from the stage, Tom stopped her.

'And now for the final award of the evening. I decided as I'm the editor that I get to hand out an award myself, and not just any award. This is the editor's award, for outstanding work.'

Grace turned to the side to see her own face larger than life on the screen. Then someone she recognised appeared, too.

'I've known Grace since she was a star pupil in class two,' Mrs Everard, her junior school teacher said. 'She was quite a chatterbox and often had to be silenced when she thought only her opinion counted, but she was a wonderful child to teach. I'm so proud of what she's achieved. Well done, Grace.'

The face on the screen changed, and she gasped when she saw it was Tyler and Flora. They chatted about her like a double act and had everyone in stitches. She glared at them both before laughing.

Finally, the last person was Joe. 'I first met Grace when she was a few hours old. She was making a lot of noise then.'

Grace smiled.

'She's grown into a wonderful woman, and such a caring person that is a credit to our market town. Recently, I've been poorly. I'm fine now.' He raised his hand to alleviate any worries. 'But I know with this young woman on my team, there is no finer person to hand the reins over to when I retire.'

Grace clenched her fists, pressing her nails into her palm, hoping to stop tears from falling. But they fell anyway. She wiped them away quickly as Joe continued. There wasn't a dry eye in the house once he'd finished.

Tom presented her with the editor's award, which was a plaque and a cheque for five hundred pounds. Grace stood next to him while Ethan took some photos.

'By the way,' Tom lowered his voice. 'When Joe retires, his job is yours. I think you've done enough to prove yourself, don't you?'

Grace found herself speechless, her smile wide as she gave him a hug. She took one more glance at everyone before stepping down into the crowd. What a night, and it wasn't over yet.

# CHAPTER FORTY-FOUR

After helping herself to the buffet, Rose was sitting next to Cedric. She wiped her mouth with a napkin and gave out a hearty sigh.

'I'm delightfully full.' She patted her tummy. 'I don't think I have room for any cake, which is a shame.'

'I agree, although I could be persuaded after a short interlude.' Cedric balled his napkin and popped it onto his plate. 'Now, while I have you to myself for a few minutes, I wanted to mention something to you.'

'Go on.' He had Rose's attention.

'You know how happy you've made me feel? My life seems complete again, and I've had a wonderful time. Well, I've been thinking about selling my cottage in Newcastle and coming back to live in Somerley. What would you say to that?'

Rose broke out into a huge smile. 'I think it's an excellent idea, and it will put Eve's mind at rest. She thinks I'm going to up sticks and move to Hexham to be nearer to you.' She leaned closer and whispered. 'And I would have done, too, if it means that we get to stay together.'

Cedric was quiet for a moment. 'You'd come to Newcastle and leave everyone behind to be with me?'

'Yes, I would. I've been thinking about it a lot. Neither of us has much time left, and I want to enjoy what's left of it.'

'I love you, Rose Pritchard. I've loved you since the day that I met you.'

'I love you, too, Cedric Brownslow, and I'm not losing you again.' She held her glass in the air. 'Here's to us. New beginnings and happy endings.'

Grace had spent the last twenty minutes chatting to people coming over to congratulate her. Finally, it was Della's turn. They'd grown closer over the past few days, now that a secret was safe between them. Grace was pleased she'd kept it to herself now.

'You've done an amazing job,' Della declared, giving her a hug. 'Despite someone sending in nasty letters, too.' She winked.

Grace smiled. 'I'm still waiting for something else to wing my way.'

'Someone will always be there to steal your thunder. Just make sure you can hit them with lightning when they do.' Della roared with laughter. 'I don't know if that even makes sense, but it sounds wonderful!'

'Sounds good to me.'

'I wanted to thank you again. For not telling anyone what I'd done and about how utterly stupid and childish I was. I just think I wanted someone to see me.'

'Honestly, it's fine. You were under a lot of stress, trying to decide what was right for you and your mum.'

'It was a difficult decision.' Della sighed. 'I hope I did the right thing.'

Della had been blown away by Somerley Heights, and the

flat and facilities. She'd told Grace it made her realise that her mum would be safer there. She'd been able to relax a little since, but equally was worried about Marianne settling in a new place.

'You did, and I'm sure Marianne will be fine,' Grace reassured her. 'You'll see.'

Grace saw Della's bottom lip trembling. 'Hey.' She grinned. 'And you bought me cupcakes! So all is well in the world.'

The smile back was reassuring. They chatted for a while longer, and then she found herself alone. She took the time to slip into the ladies'. When she saw herself in the mirror, she was thankful she had. Her hair was sticking up in so many places where she'd been nervously running her hand through it, her makeup barely there.

She freshened up, adding lipstick and perfume, and then went back out into the main hall. Tyler was standing on the side wall, his back against a window sill. He smiled when she approached him, and her stomach fluttered in response.

'I have something for you,' he said, slipping his hand inside his jacket. He pulled out a tiny white envelope.

'Another one without a stamp?' she queried. 'It's a bit late now, though.'

'This one is for you. It's a note, really, rather than a letter.'

She took it from him. 'Are you blushing, Tyler Walker?'

'I might be after you've read it.'

Confused, she opened it to find a card. It had a picture of a puppy and a rabbit sitting in a hammock together. After a quick glance at him, she read the message inside.

*I've really enjoyed getting to know you better these past few weeks. I can't stop thinking about you, so would you like to go out with me one evening?*

'Oh!' She looked at him properly this time.

'Oh?'

'It's just... I thought you'd never ask.'

'Well, I know how partial you are to a letter, so... how about tomorrow, if you're free? Or any other night if you're busy. I assume you have lots of evening events to go to and—'

'Tomorrow is good.' She stopped him.

'Excellent.' He grinned. 'Do you fancy The Caramel Leaf or the Italian down the road?'

'The Italian, please.'

'Great. I'll book a table. Is seven too early?'

'Seven is fine, but what about this evening? The night is young. We could go for a drink afterwards.'

His smile told her all she needed to know. She waggled an empty glass at him. 'You could get me a refill first, though. I am gasping.'

Grace watched him as he walked away, a huge rush of lust washing over her. Tyler was everything Liam wasn't. It was time to learn to love someone else. She had a feeling she was going to enjoy herself very much.

'What are you smiling about?' Flora came to stand with her.

'I've got a date. Tyler's asked me out.'

'At last.' Flora's tone was exaggerated.

Grace smiled, then she laughed. She threw an arm around Flora's shoulder. 'What would I do without you?'

Eve and Mack went around the room saying their goodbyes before finally getting out into the night. It was cool, and Mack put an arm around her as they walked to the car. When they reached it, Eve noticed there was something on the windscreen, held in place on the passenger side by the wiper.

'What's that?' She pointed to it once they drew closer.

Mack shrugged. 'I think it's addressed to you.'

She frowned, reaching for it and opening it. Inside was a piece of paper.

*A is for adorable.*
*B is for beautiful.*
*C is for Cute.*
*D is for delightful.*
*E is for excellent.*

She gazed up at him. 'You've gone through the whole alphabet?' She carried on reading.

*K is for killer smile.*
*L is for loving.*
*M is for marvellous.*

'It took me ages to think of something for every letter,' he said. 'Well, nearly all of them.'

Eve read on.

*P is for perfect.*
*Q is for Queen!*
*R is for reliable.*
*S is for seductive.*
*T is for tantalising.*

She burst into raucous laughter.

'I'm so *glad* I came back to Somerley,' he replied.

'Well, me, too.' She held her breath. He hadn't mentioned anything about leaving for a while. Did this mean…?

'I haven't been this happy in a long time.' Mack threaded his fingers through her own. 'So, how would you feel if I stayed here for good?'

'I would like that very much.' She pulled him closer, gazing into the eyes of the man she loved, pleased they'd been given a second chance. She thought how apt the name for Grace's project was. One letter.

L is for Love.

Because love really does make the world go round.

## ALSO BY MARCIE STEELE

The Somerley Collection
Stirred with Love
Secrets, Lies and Love
Second Chances at Love
Moving On

The Hope Street Series
The Man Across the Street, Book 1
Coming Home to Hope Street, Book 2

# ACKNOWLEDGMENTS

To my friends Alison Niebierszczanski, Imogen Clark, Louise Ross, Talli Roland, Caroline Mitchell, and Sharon Sant. Thanks for all the coffee, cake and chats!

Many thanks also to anyone who has emailed me, messaged me, chatted to me on Facebook and told me how much they have enjoyed reading this book. I've been genuinely blown away with all kinds of niceness and support from you all. A writer's job is often a lonely one but I feel I truly have friends everywhere.

# ABOUT THE AUTHOR

Marcie Steele is a pen name. I'm Mel Sherratt and ever since I can remember, I've been a meddler of words. Born and raised in Stoke-on-Trent, Staffordshire, I used the city as a backdrop for my first novel, Taunting the Dead, and it went on to be a Kindle number one bestseller and the overall number eight UK Kindle bestselling book of 2012. Since then, I've written twenty-six books and sold over two million copies.

As Mel, I like writing about fear and emotion – the cause and effect of crime – what makes a character do something. Working as a housing officer for eight years also gave me the background to create a fictional estate full of good and bad characters (think *Brassic* meets *Coronation Street*.)

But I'm a romantic at heart and have always wanted to write about characters that are not necessarily involved in the darker side of life. I like to write about love, romance, friendship, family, secrets and lies in everyday life - feel good factor with humour and heart.

Coffee, cakes and friends are three of my favourite things, hence writing under the name of Marcie Steele too. I can often be found sitting in a coffee shop, sipping a cappuccino and eating a chocolate chip cookie, either catching up with friends or writing on my laptop.

Copyright © Marcie Steele 2023

All rights reserved.

The right of Marcie Steele to be identified as the author of this work has been asserted in accordance with the Copyright, Designs and Patents Act 1988. All rights reserved in all media.

No part of this publication may be reproduced, stored in or transmitted into any retrieval system, in any form, or by any means (electronic, mechanical, photocopying, recording or otherwise) without the prior written permission of the publisher. Any person who does any unauthorised act in relation to this publication may be liable to criminal prosecution and civil claims for damages.

This is a work of fiction. Names, characters, businesses, places, events and incidents are either the products of the author's imagination or used in a fictitious manner. Any resemblance to actual persons, living or dead, or actual events is purely coincidental.

Cover design copyright © Marcie Steele

Printed in Great Britain
by Amazon